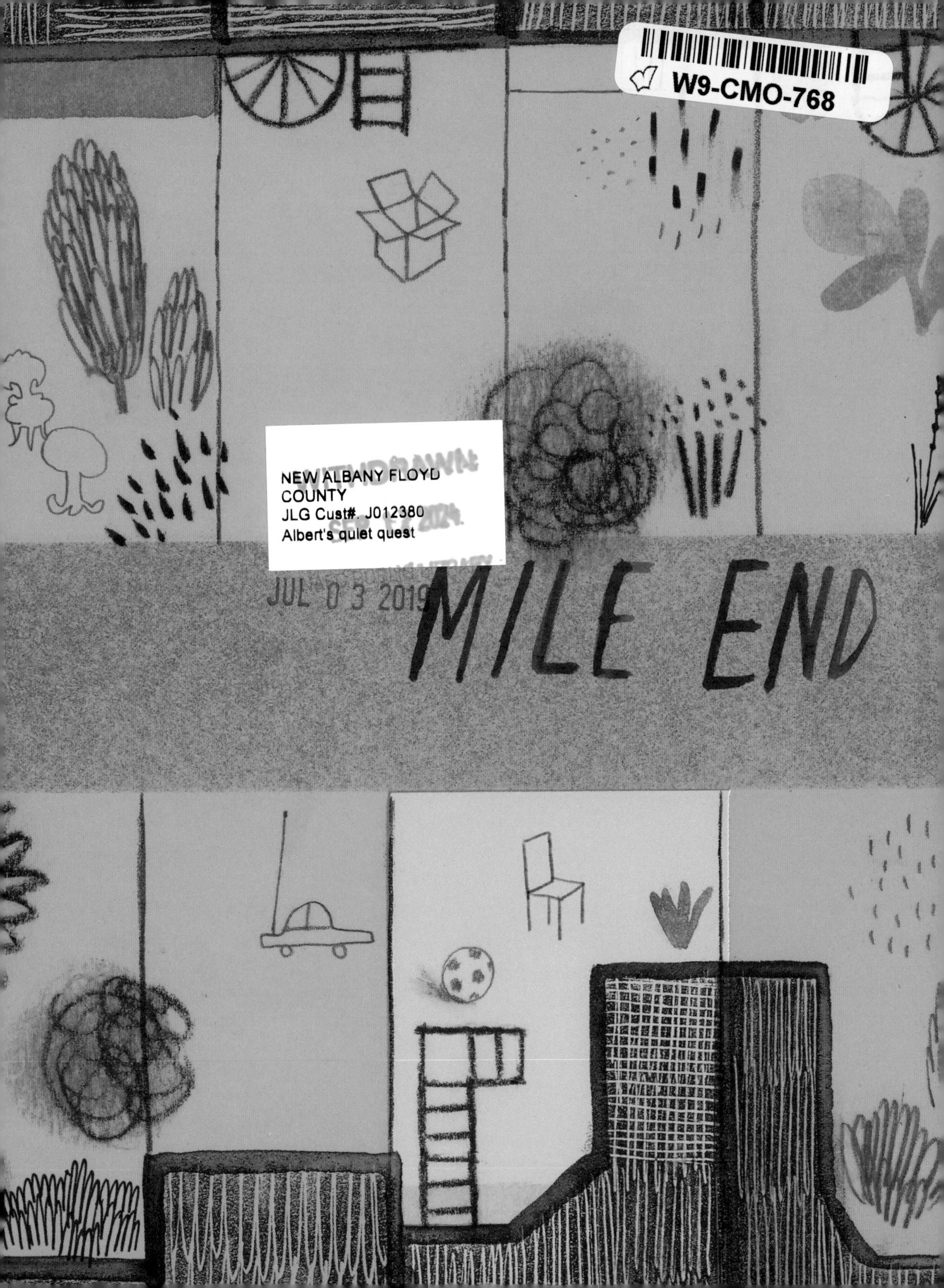
MILE END

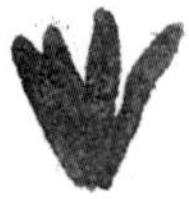

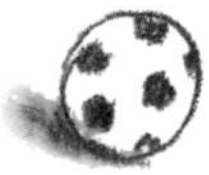

To Arnaud. – I.A.

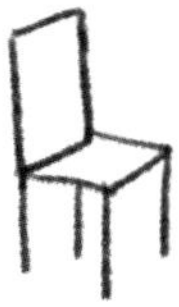



Tundra Books, an imprint of Penguin Random House Canada Young Readers,
a Penguin Random House Company



Library and Archives Canada Cataloguing in Publication
Arsenault, Isabelle, 1978–, author, illustrator
Albert's quiet quest/ Isabelle Arsenault.
Issued in print and electronic formats.
ISBN 978-1-101-91762-6 (hardcover).--ISBN 978-1-101-91764-0 (EPUB)
I. Title.
PS8601.R7538A79 2019 jC813'.6 C2018-902943-9 C2018-902961-7

Published simultaneously in the United States of America
by Random House Books for Young Readers

Edited by Tara Walker and Maria Modugno
Designed by Isabelle Arsenault and Kelly Hill
The artwork in this book was rendered in pencils, watercolor and ink
with digital coloration in Photoshop.
Handlettering by Isabelle Arsenault

Printed and bound in China
www.penguinrandomhouse.ca

1 2 3 4 5 23 22 21 20 19

tundra | Penguin Random House
TUNDRA BOOKS

A Mile End Kids Story

# ALBERT'S QUIET QUEST

Words and pictures by

ISABELLE ARSENAULT

TUNDRA

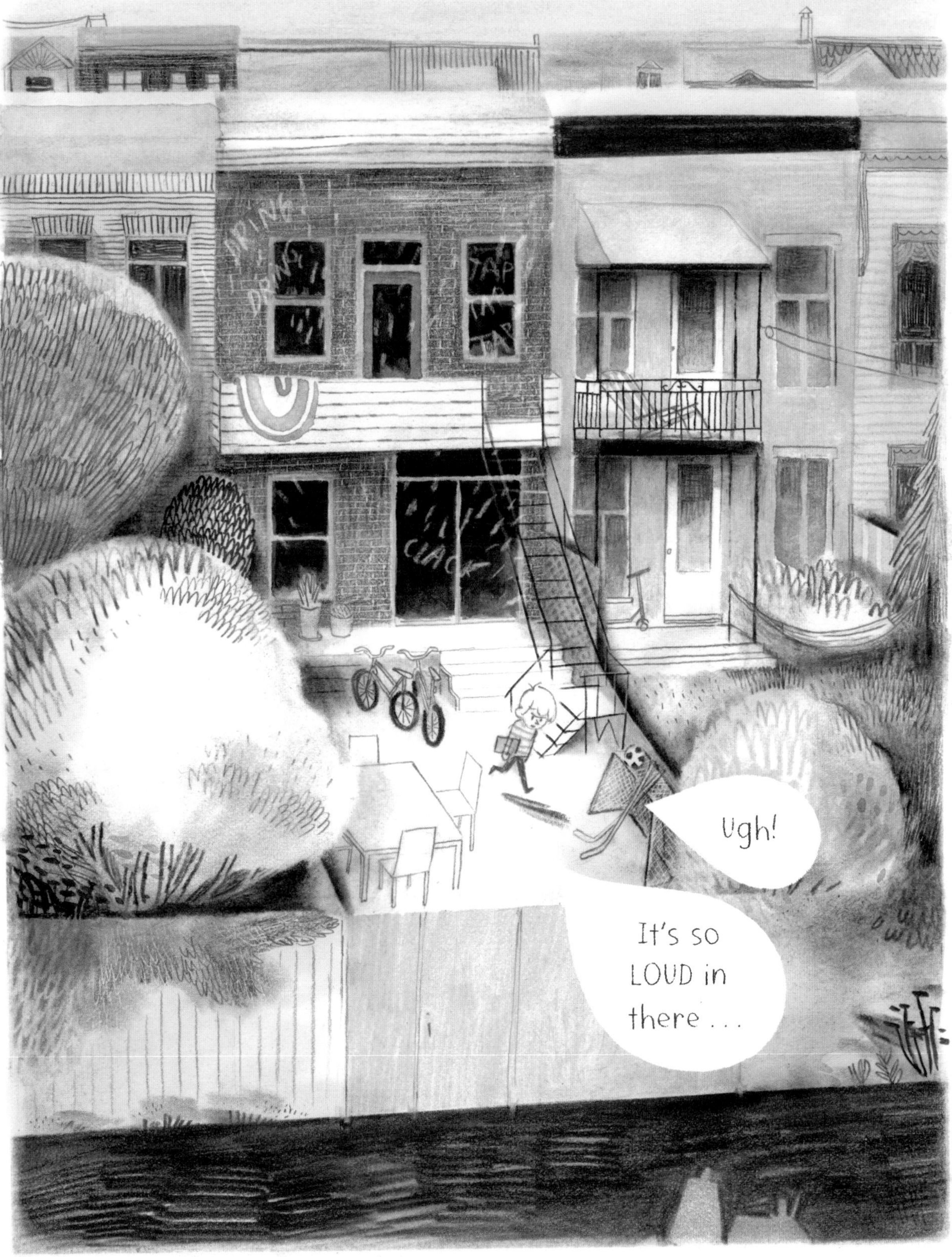
DRING!
TAP
CLACK
Ugh!
It's so LOUD in there . . .

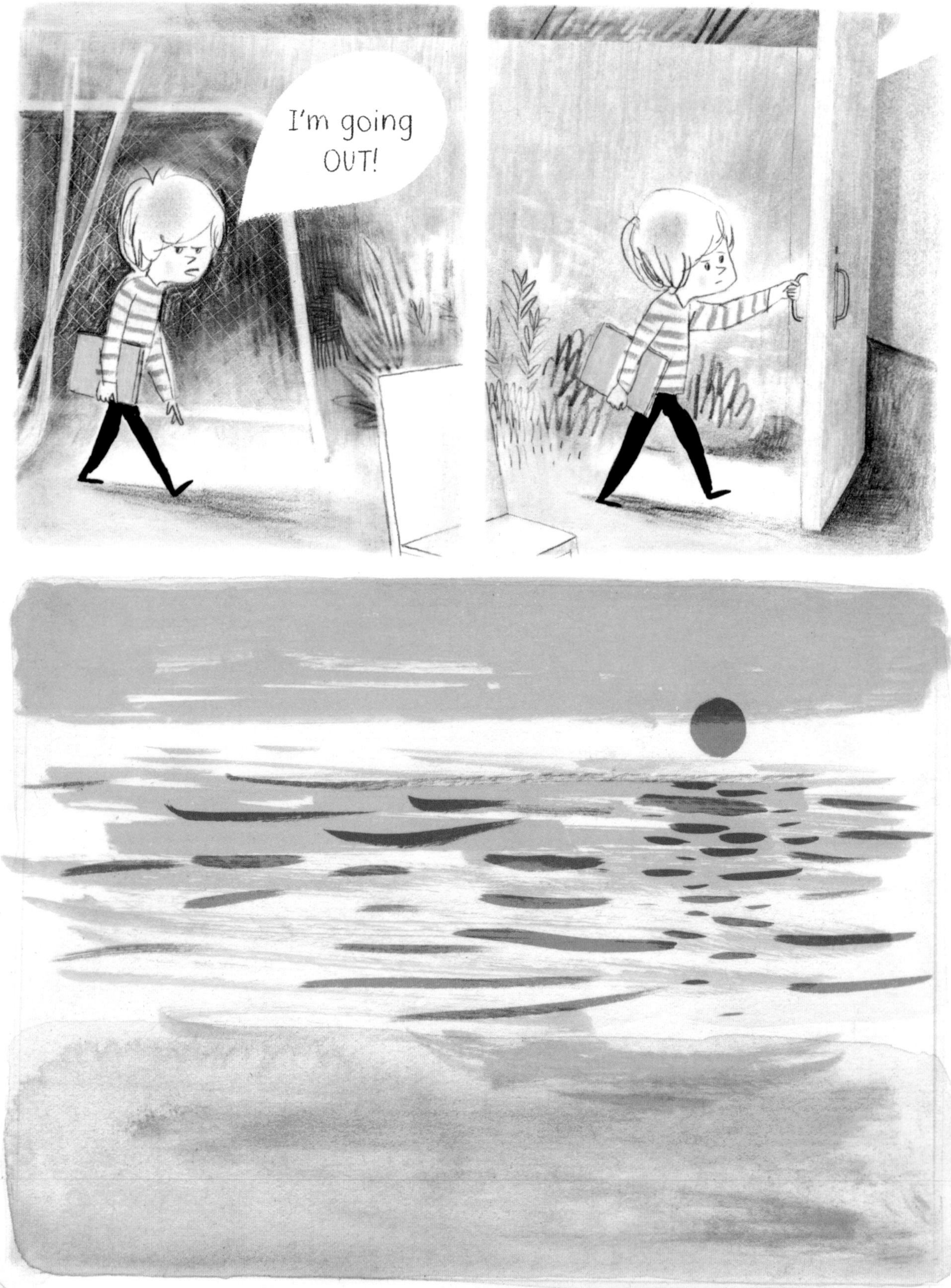
I'm going OUT!

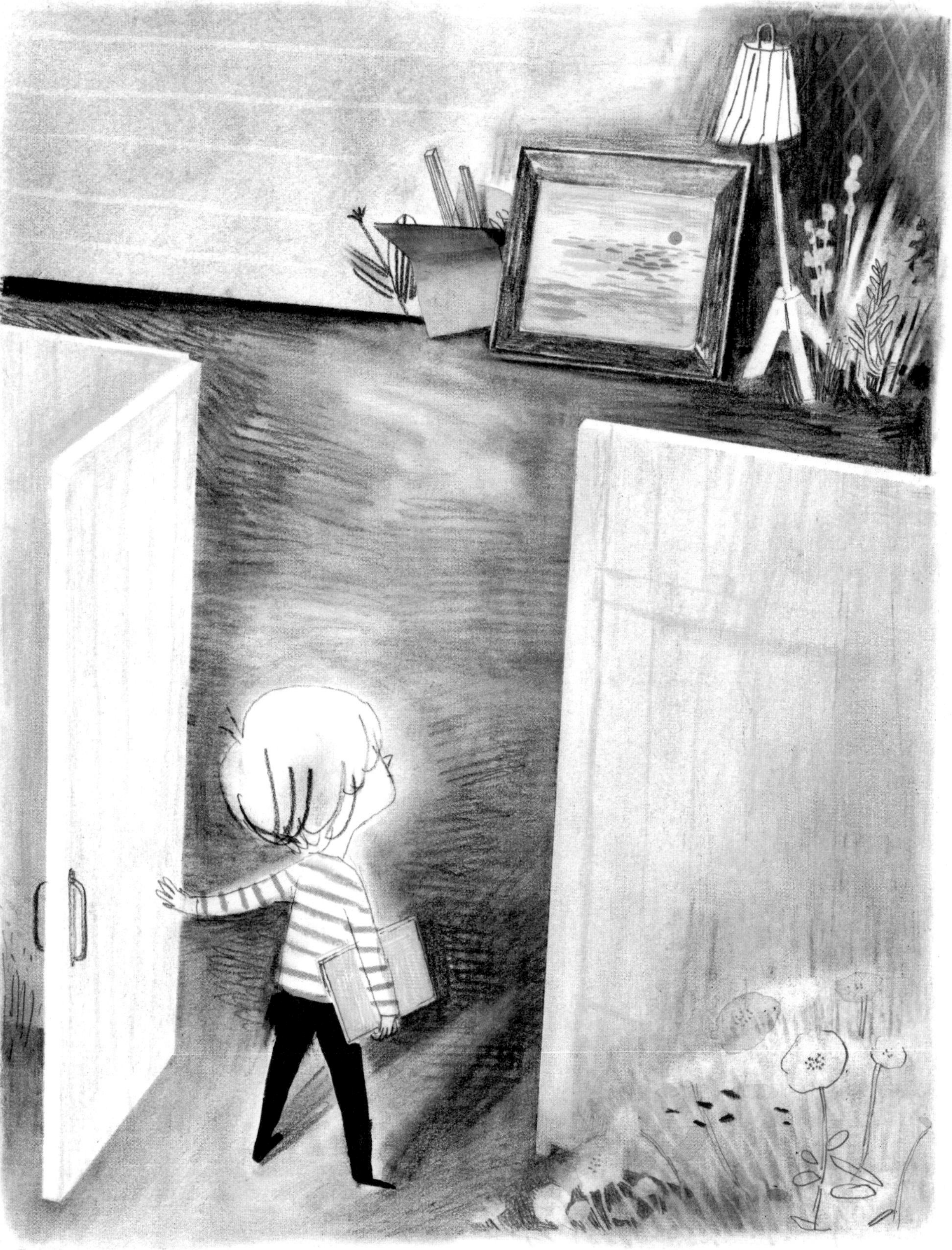

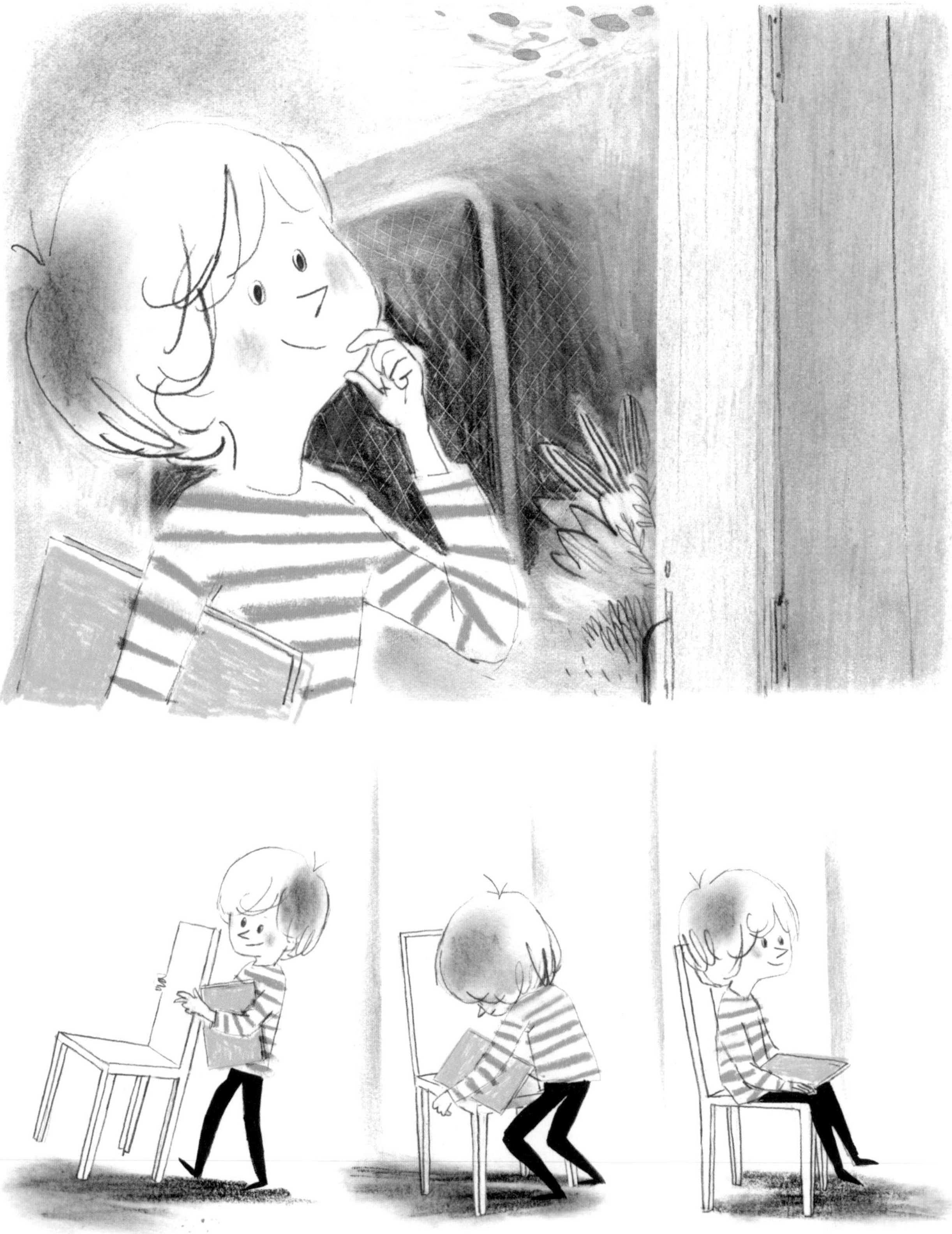

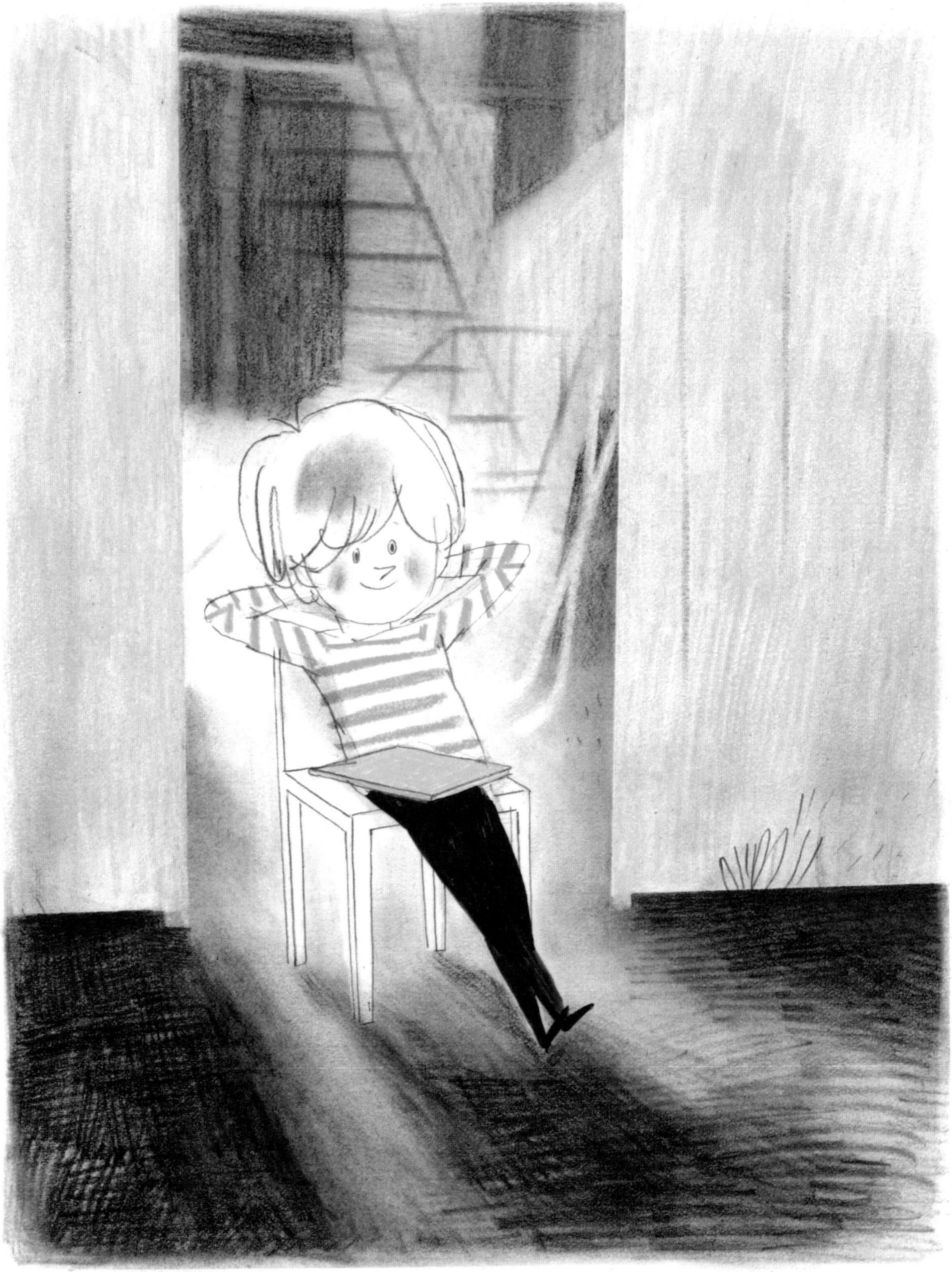

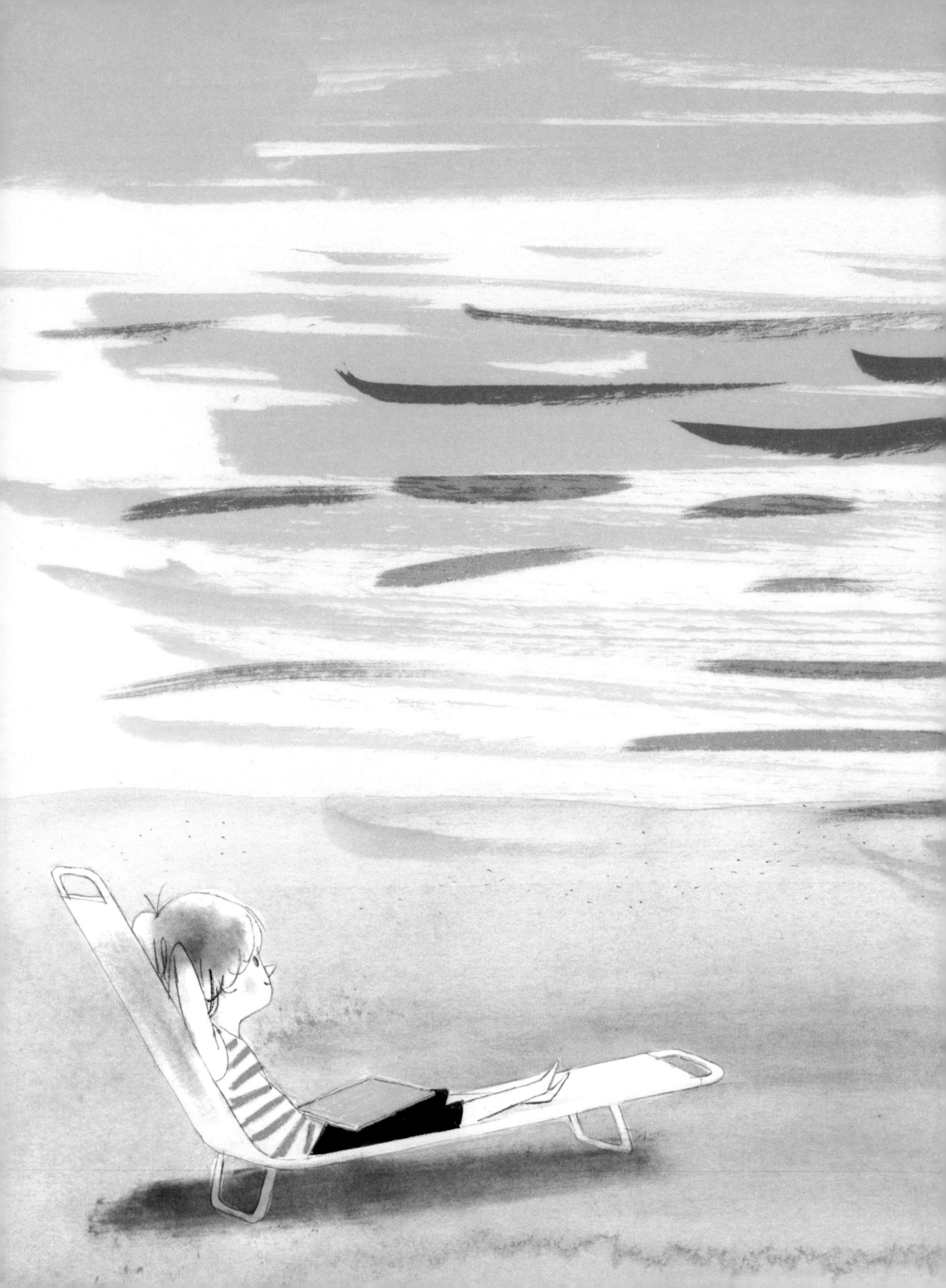

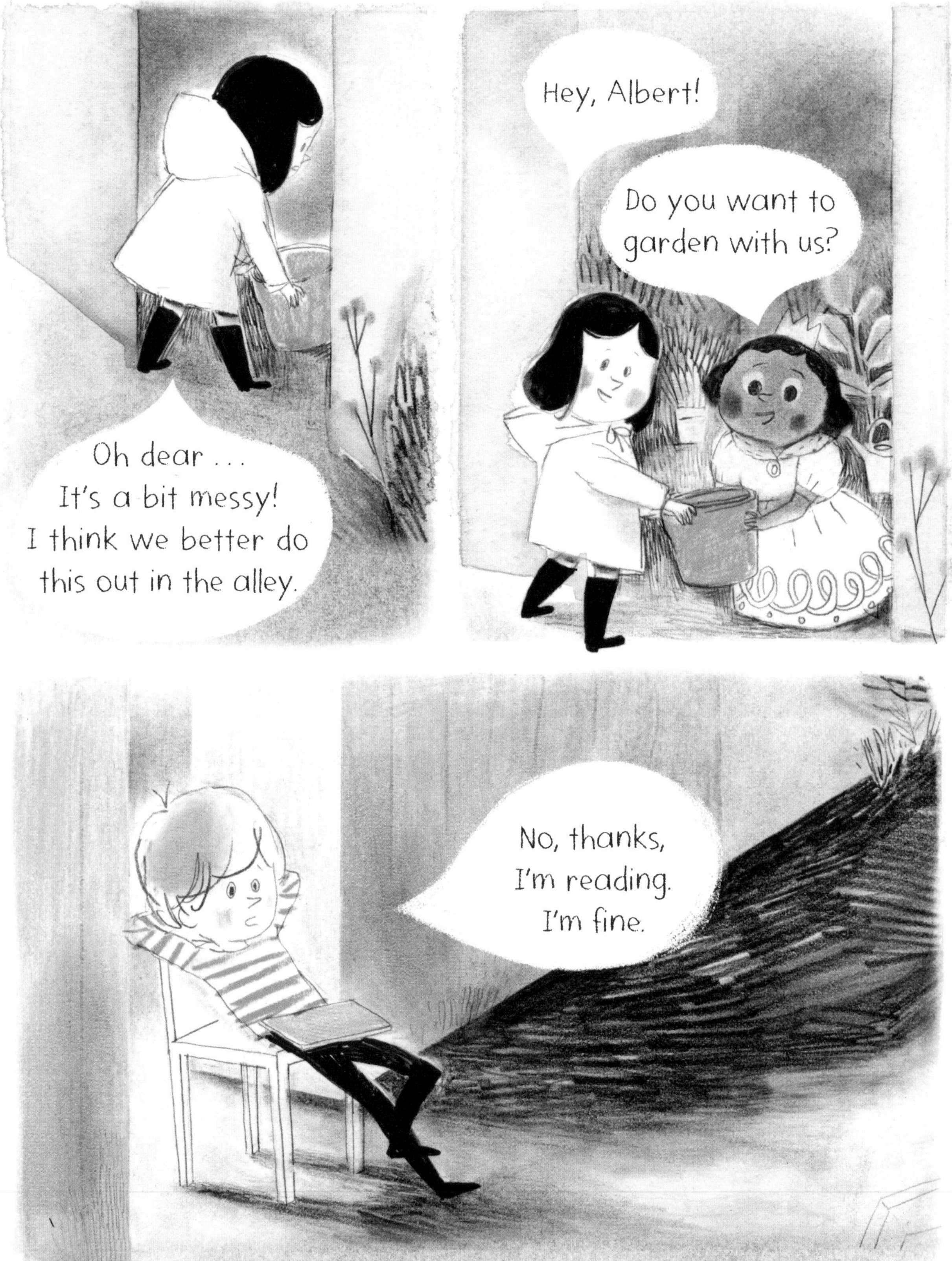

Oh dear . . . It's a bit messy! I think we better do this out in the alley.
Hey, Albert!
Do you want to garden with us?
No, thanks, I'm reading. I'm fine.

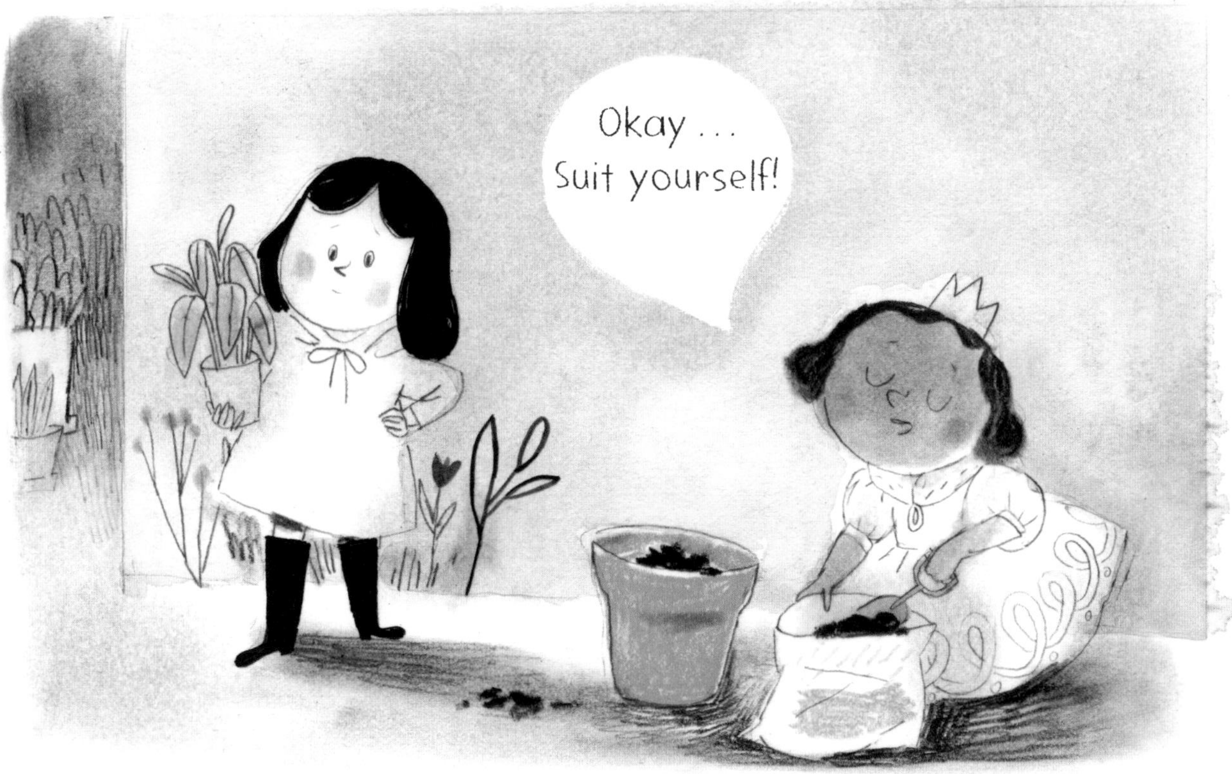
Okay . . .
Suit yourself!

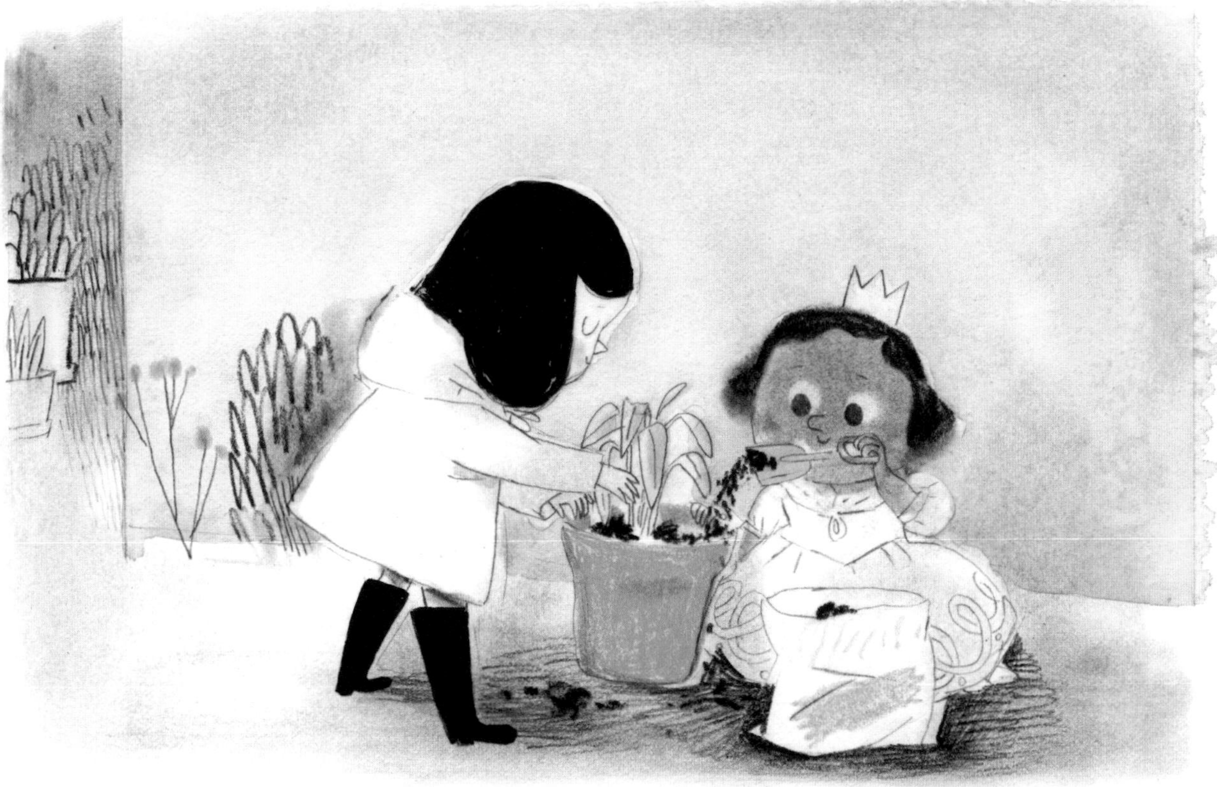

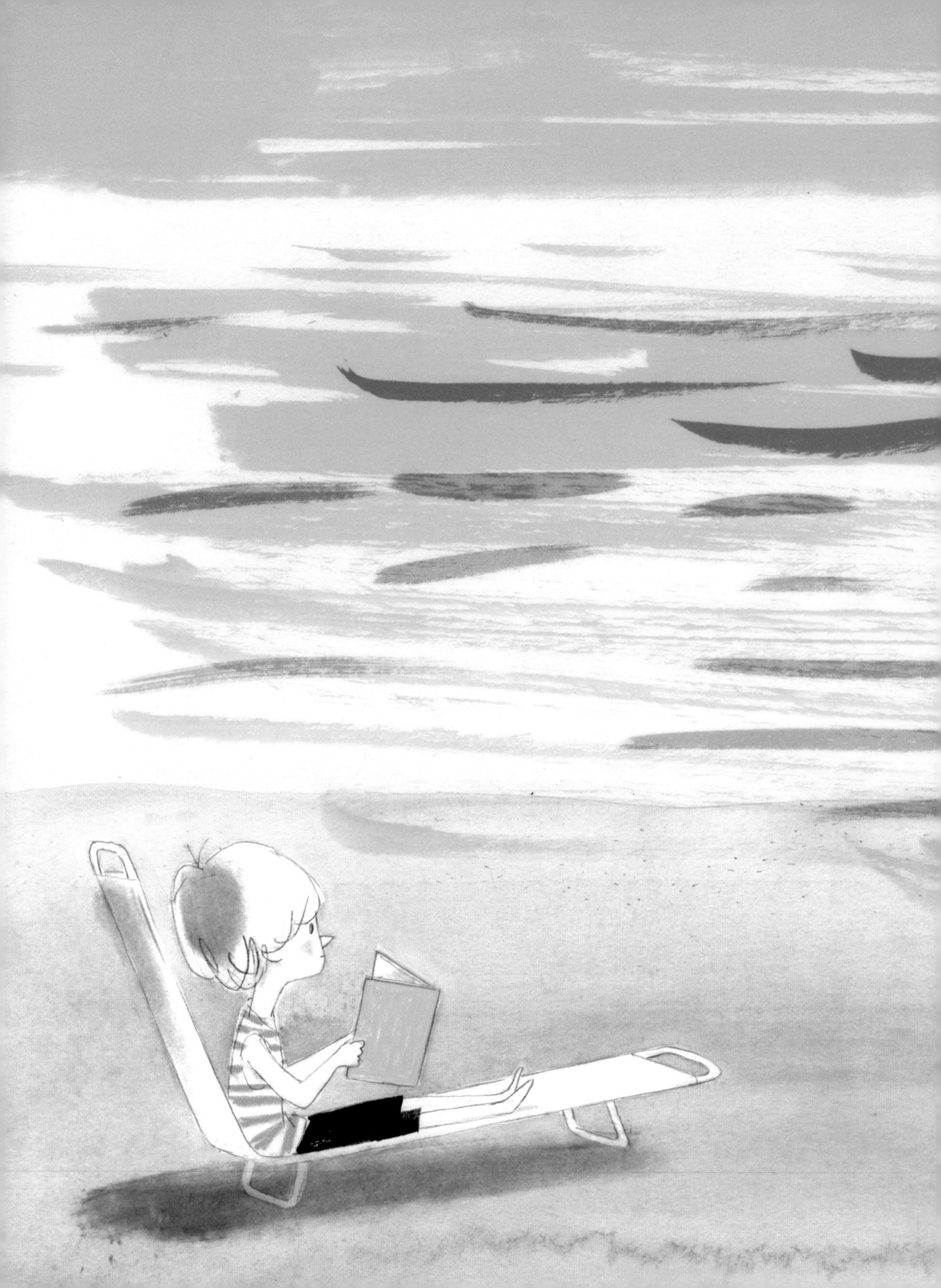

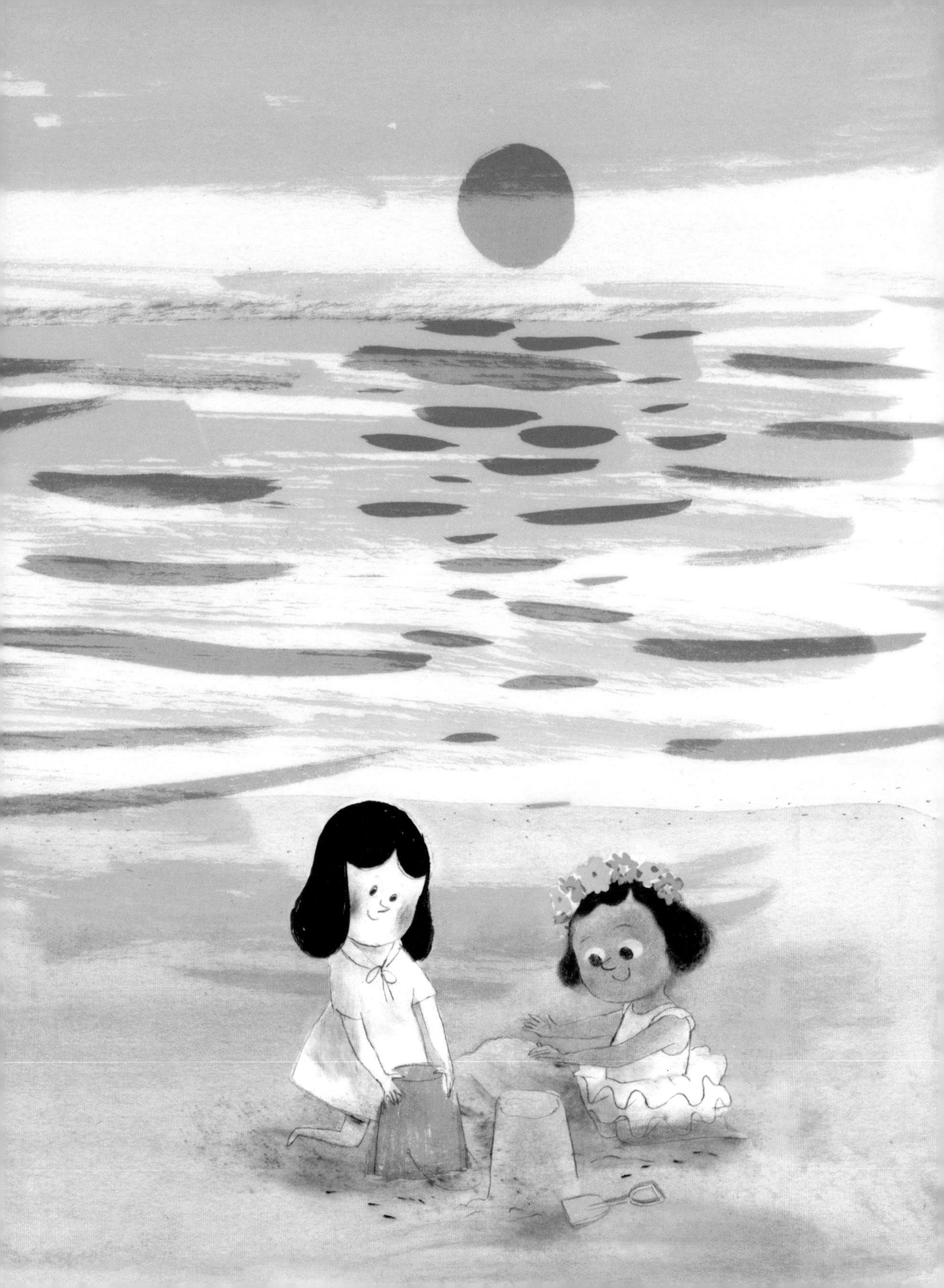

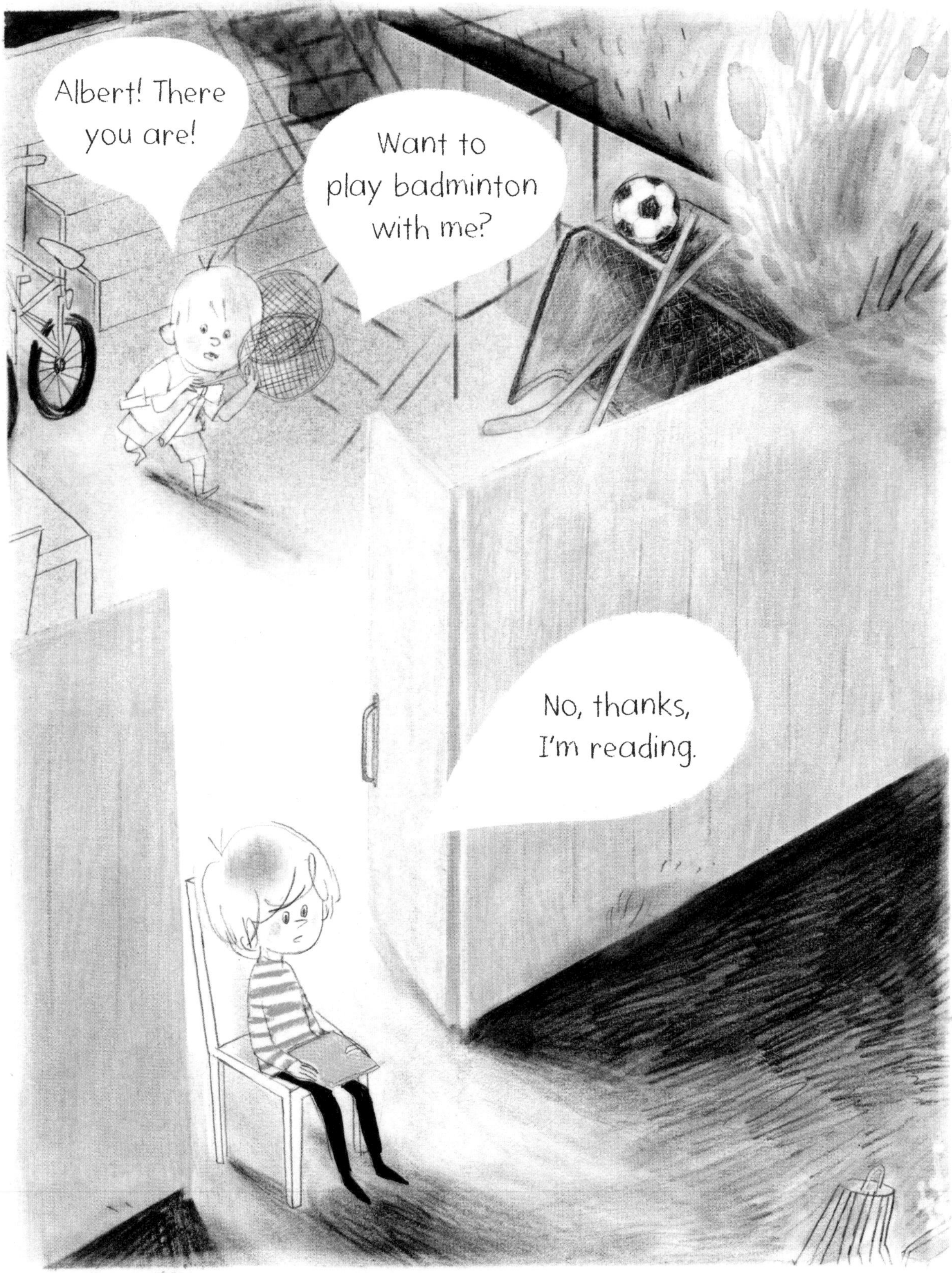
Albert! There you are!
Want to play badminton with me?
No, thanks, I'm reading.

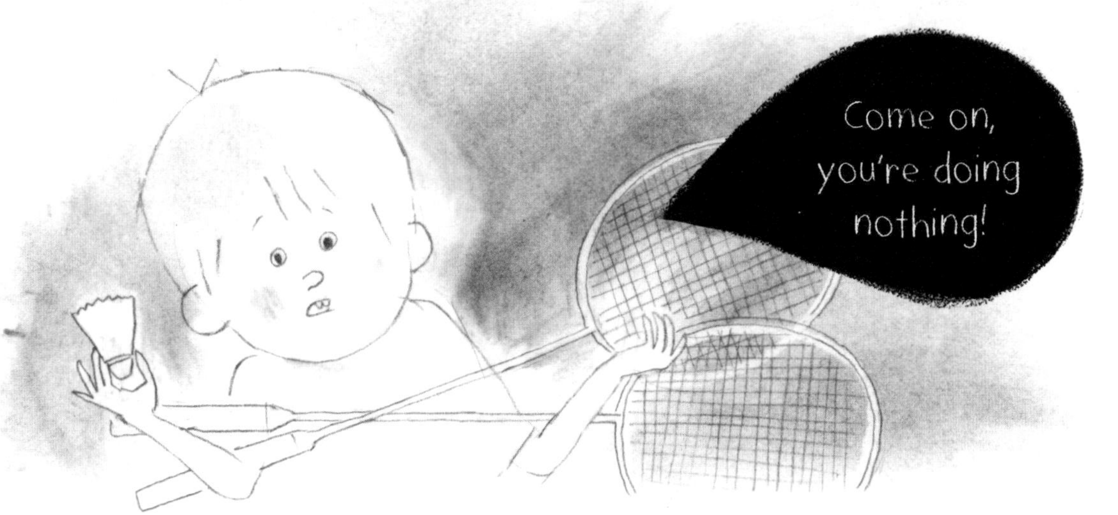
Come on, you're doing nothing!

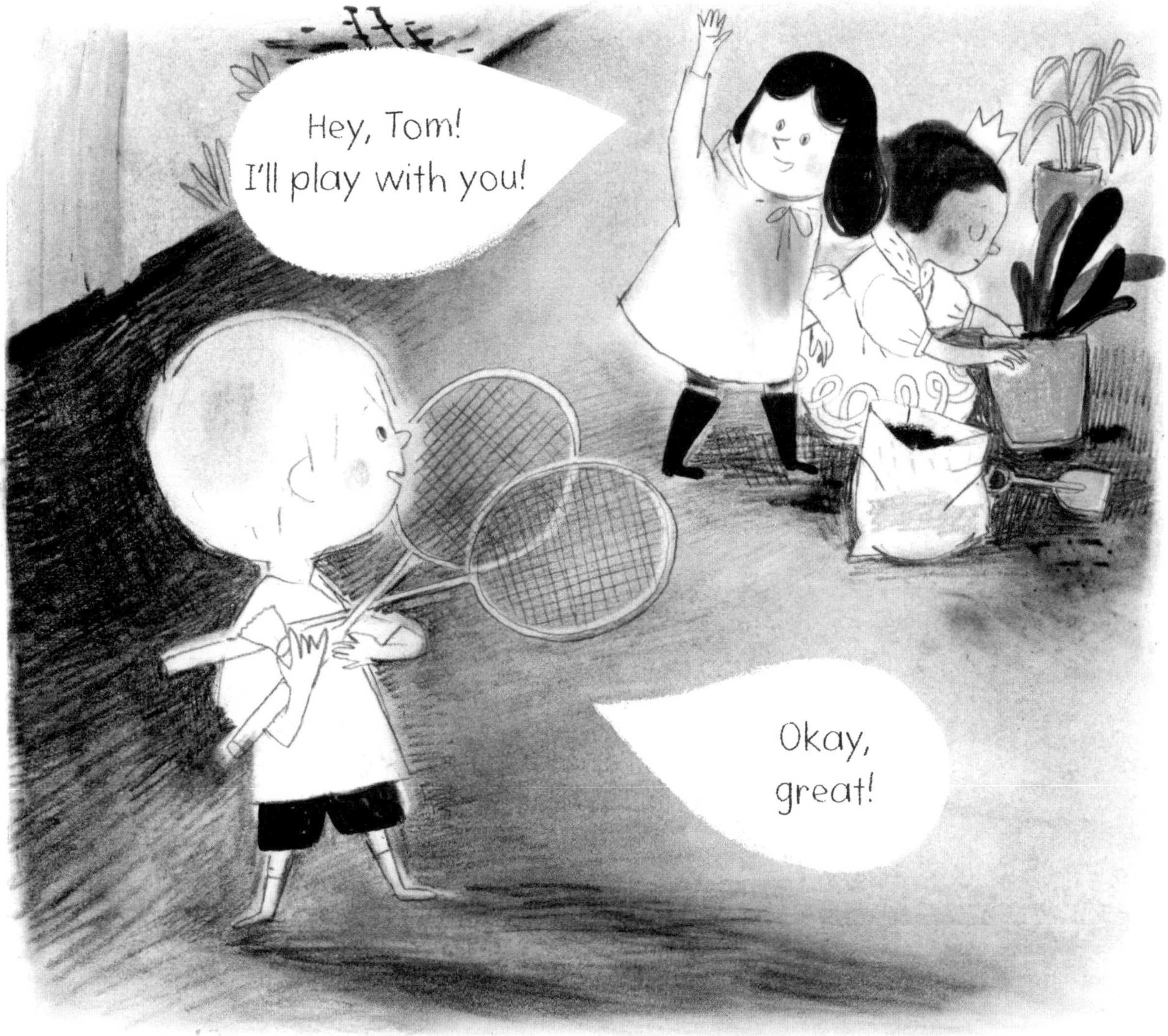
Hey, Tom! I'll play with you!
Okay, great!

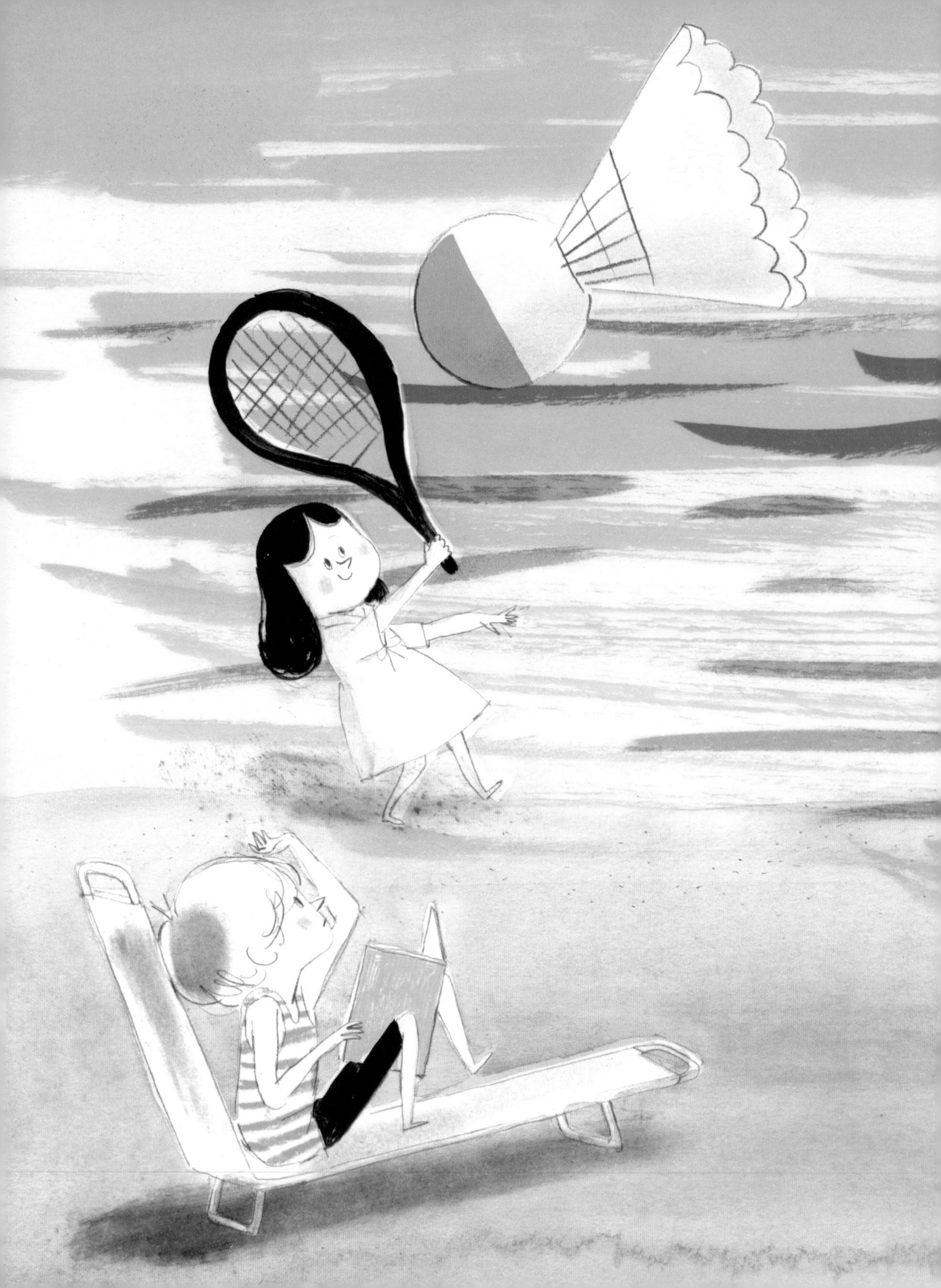

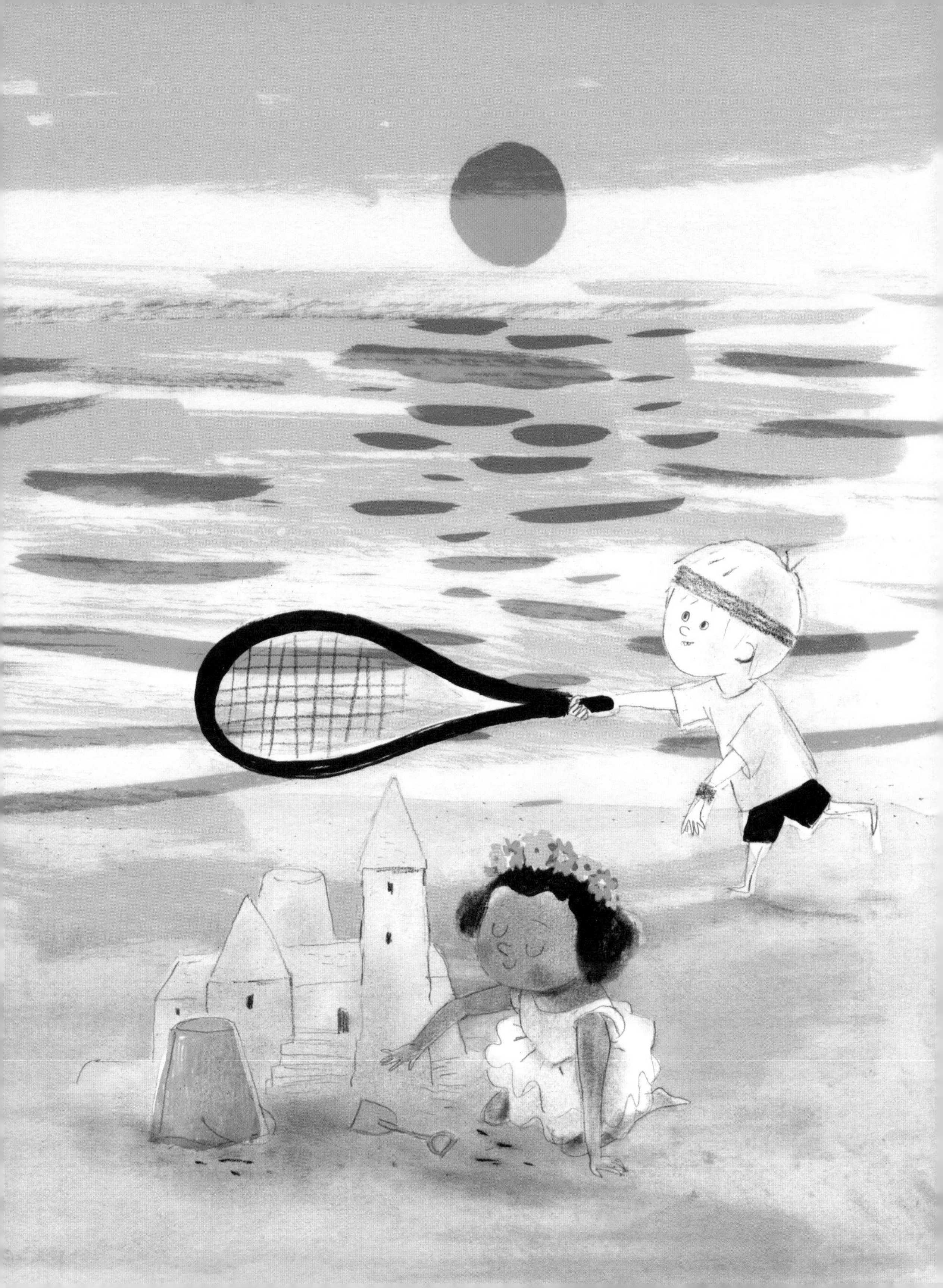

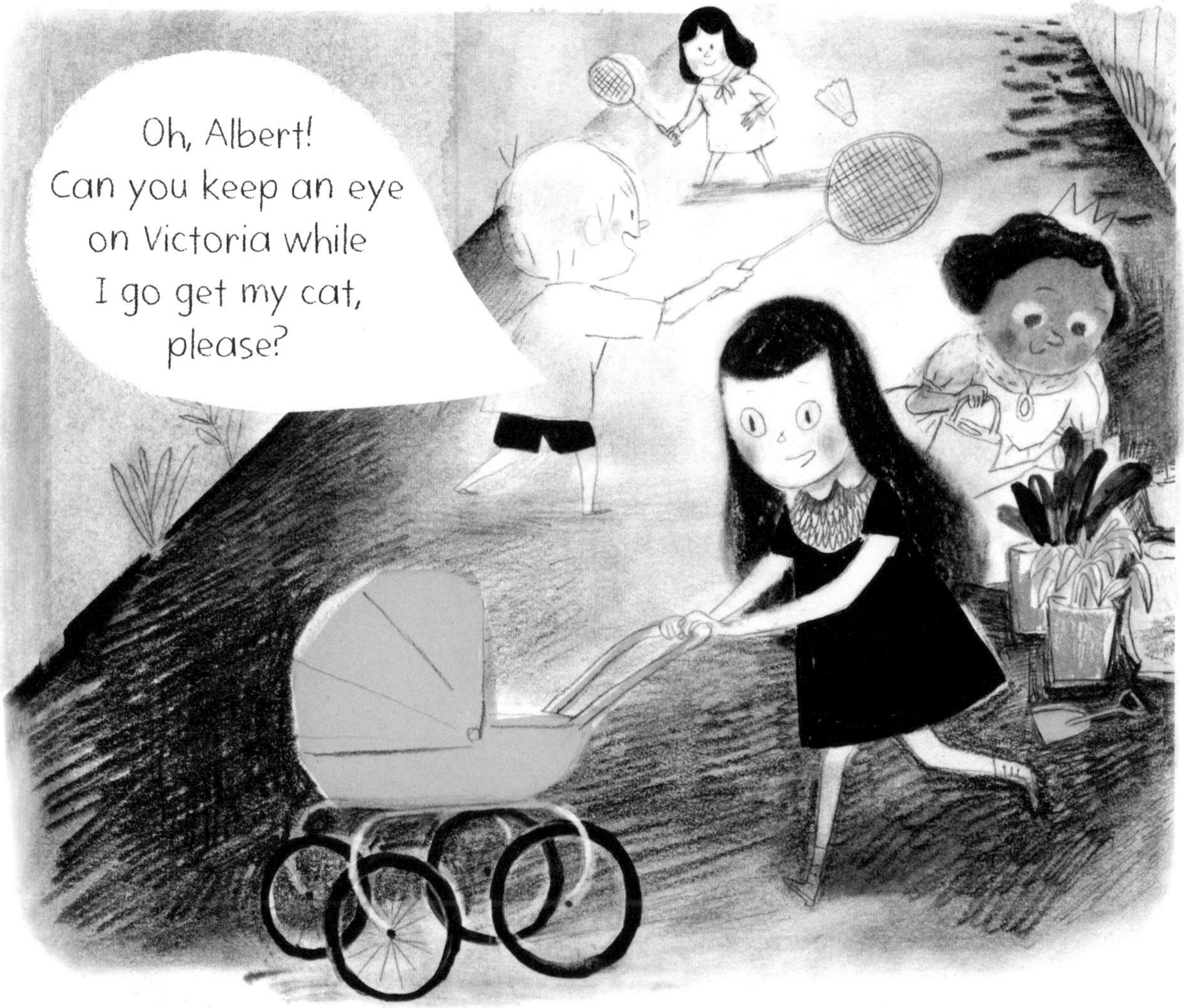
Oh, Albert! Can you keep an eye on Victoria while I go get my cat, please?

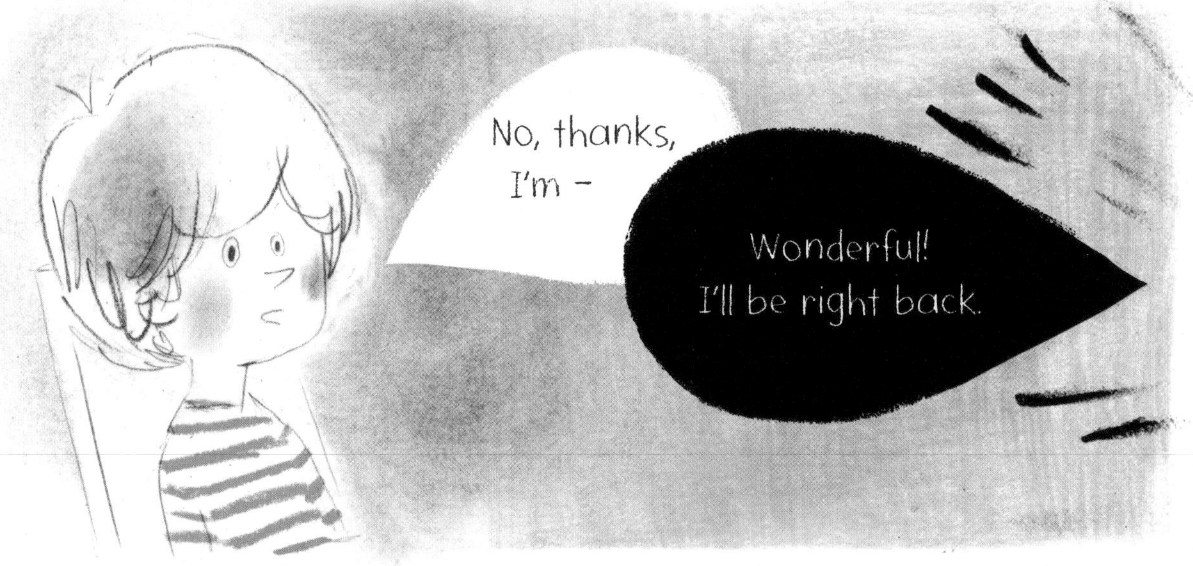
No, thanks, I'm –
Wonderful! I'll be right back.

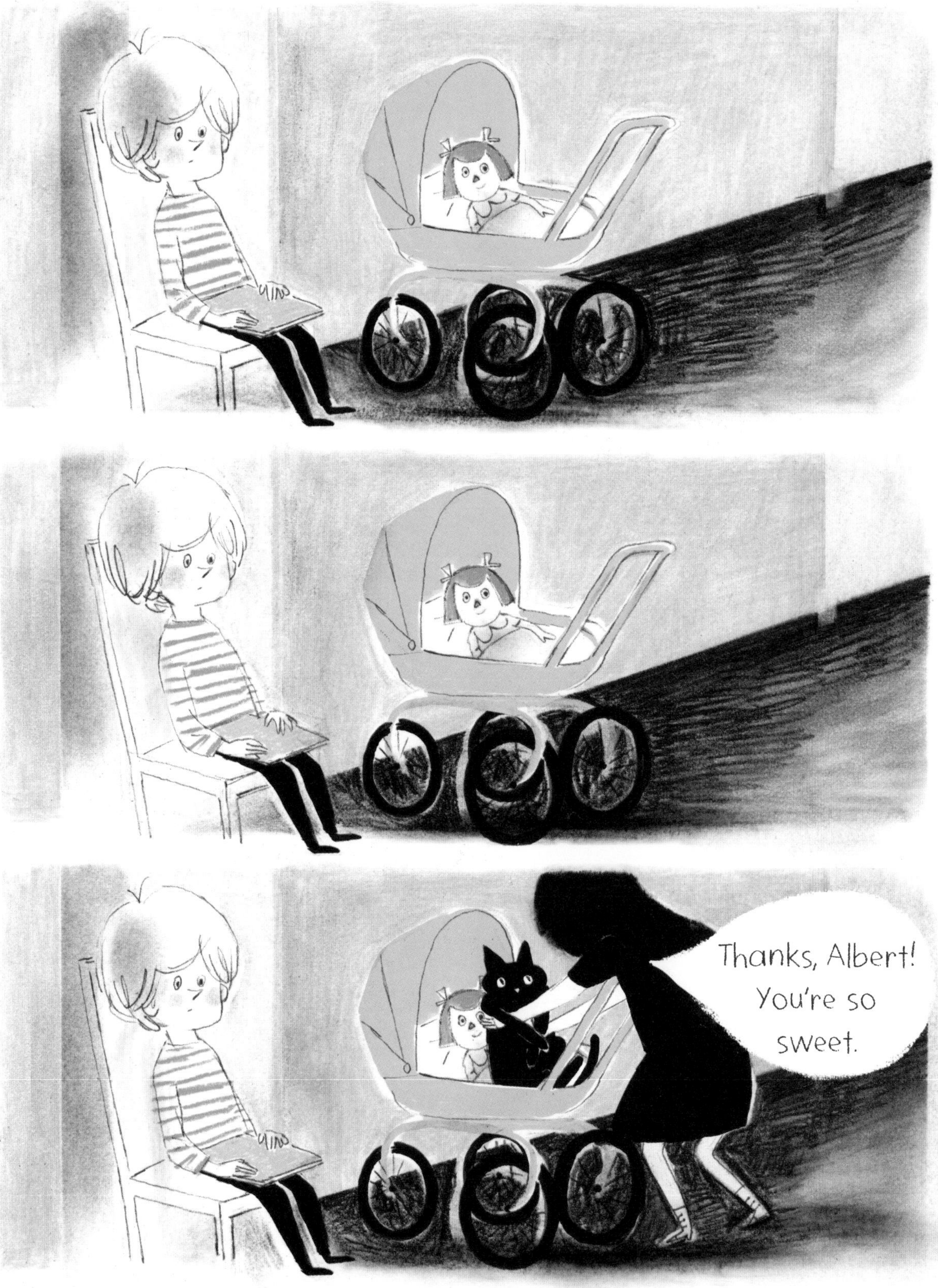
Thanks, Albert! You're so sweet.

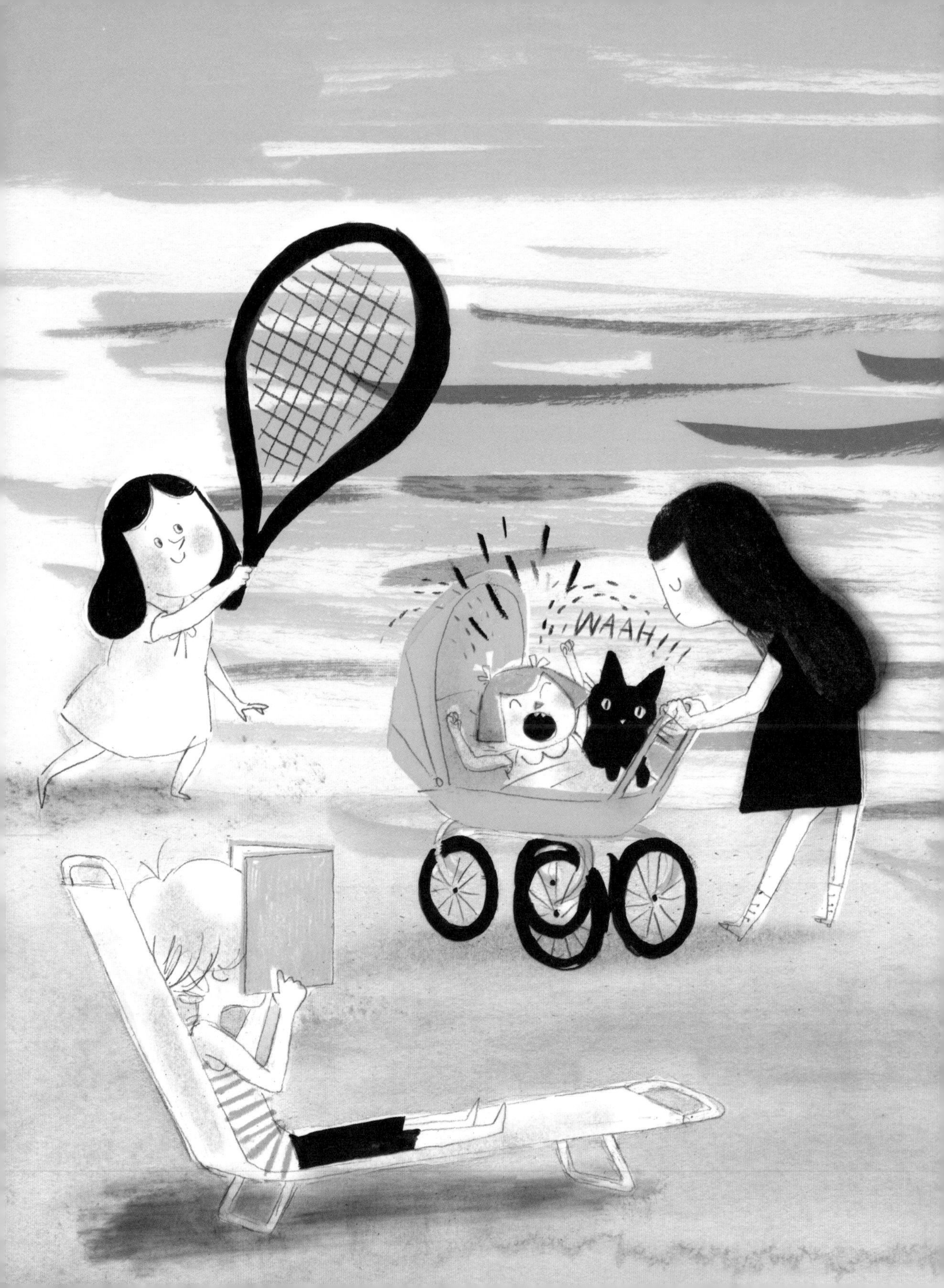
WAAH

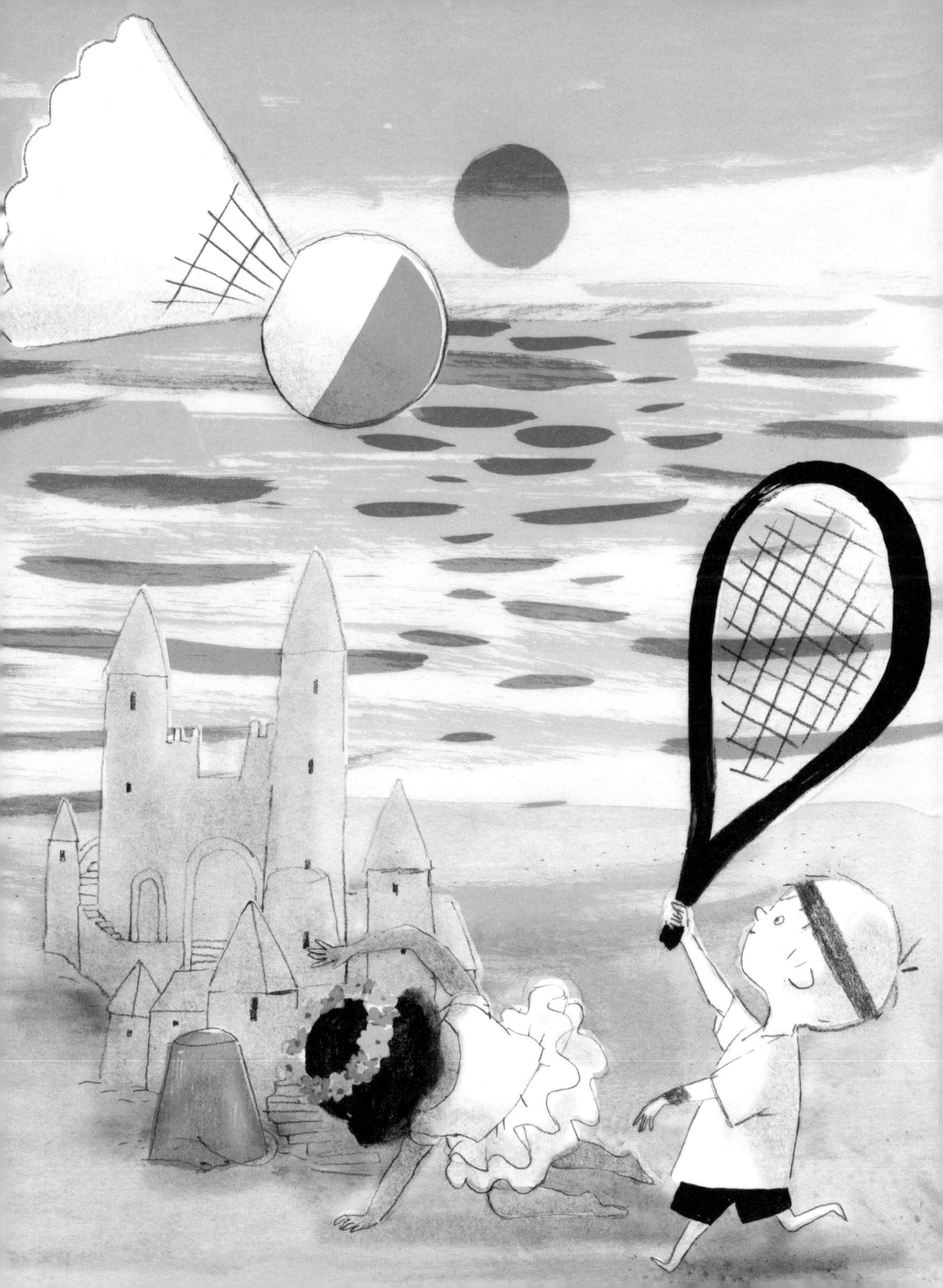

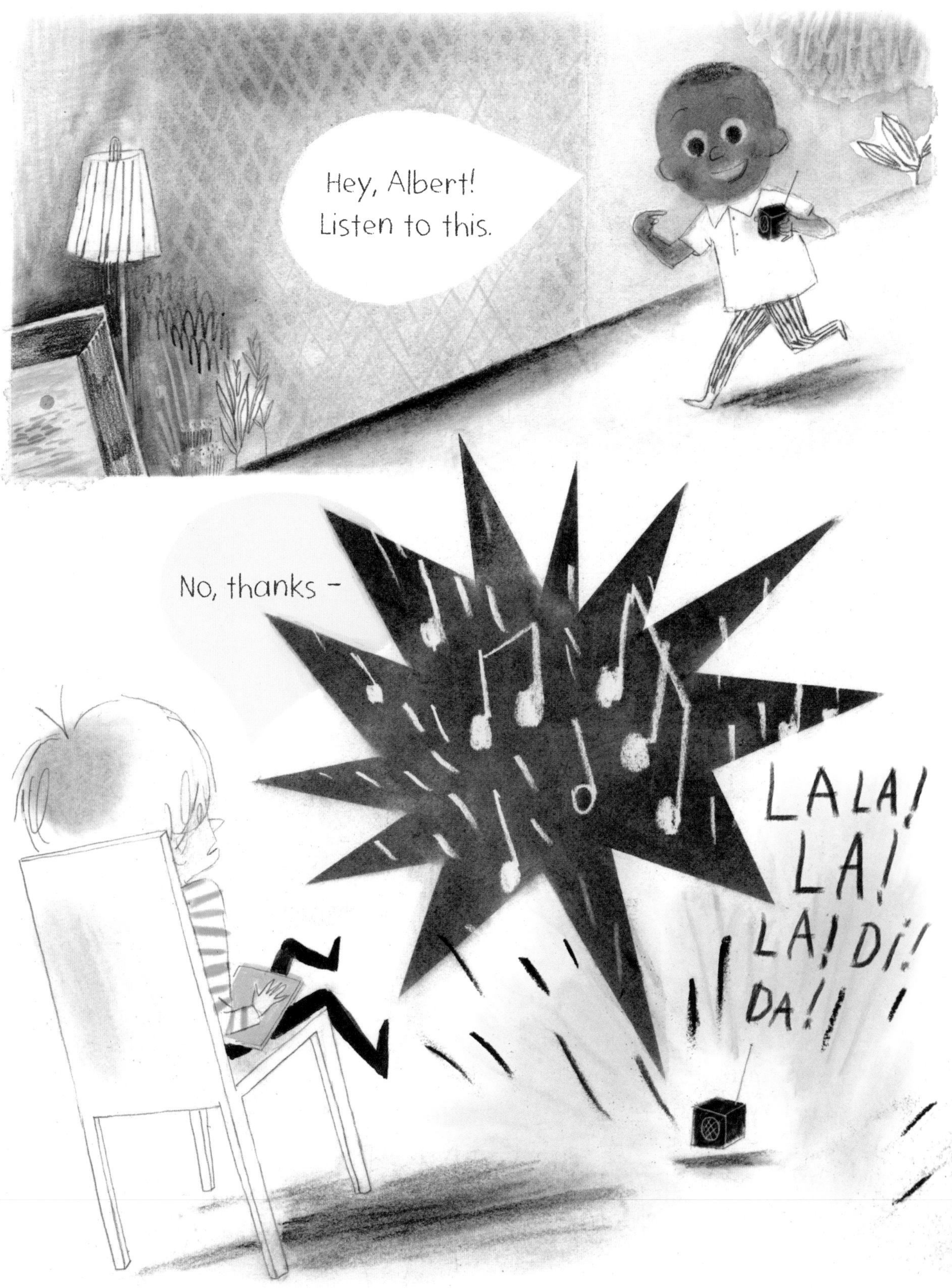
Hey, Albert!
Listen to this.
No, thanks -
LA LA!
LA!
LA! DI!
DA!

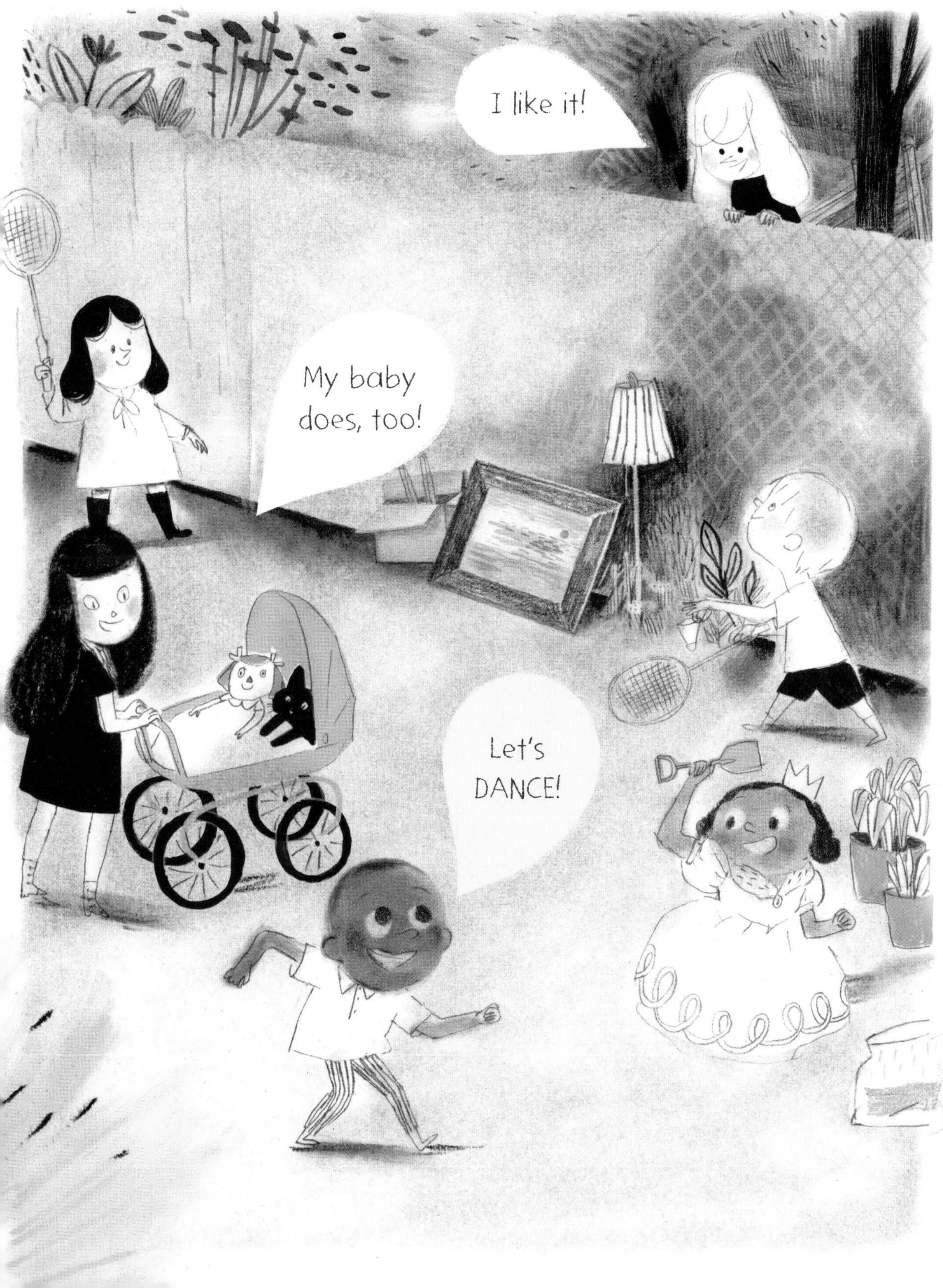
I like it!
My baby does, too!
Let's DANCE!

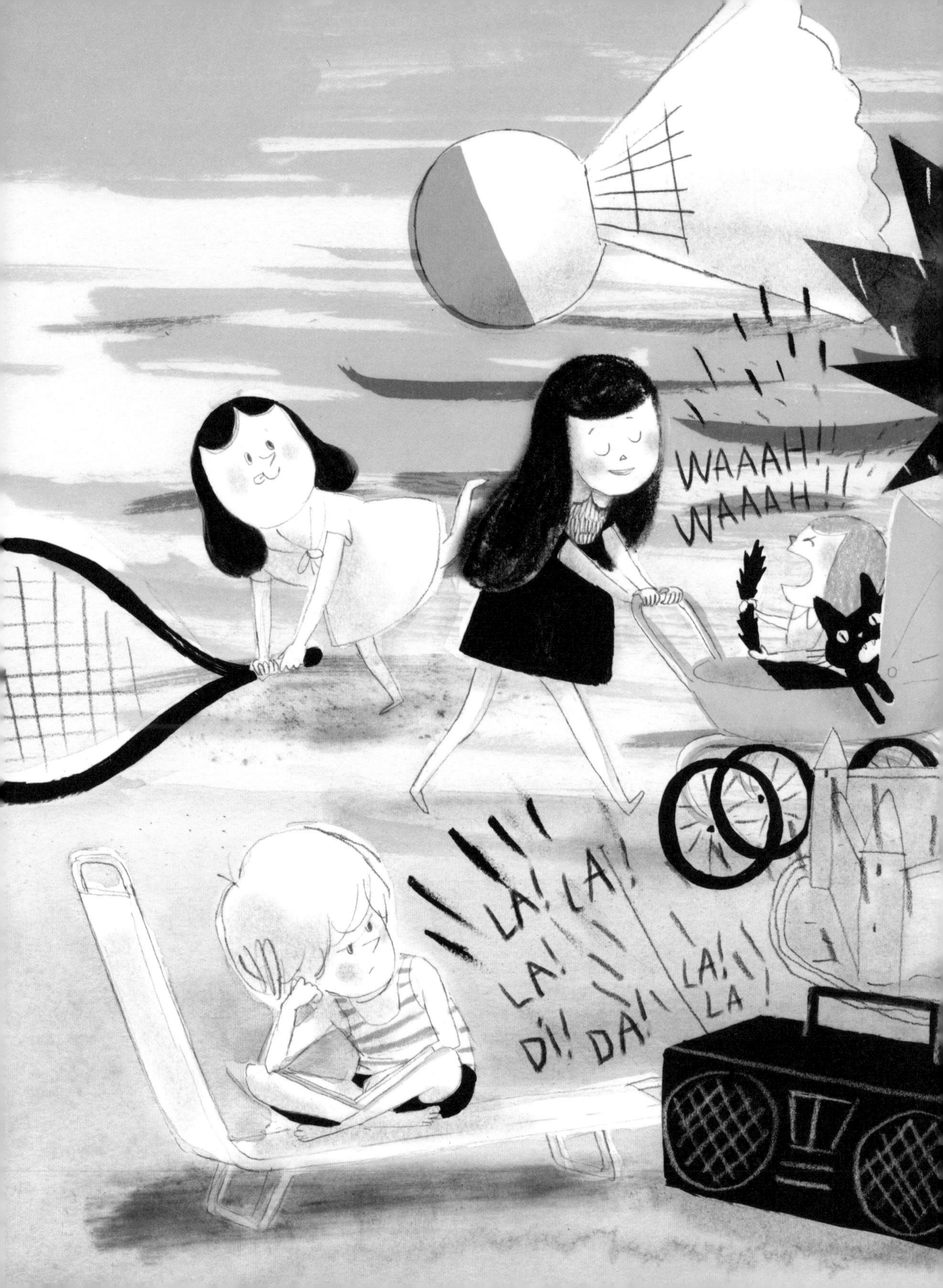
WAAAH!!
WAAAH!!
LA! LA!
LA!
DI! DA!
LA!
LA!

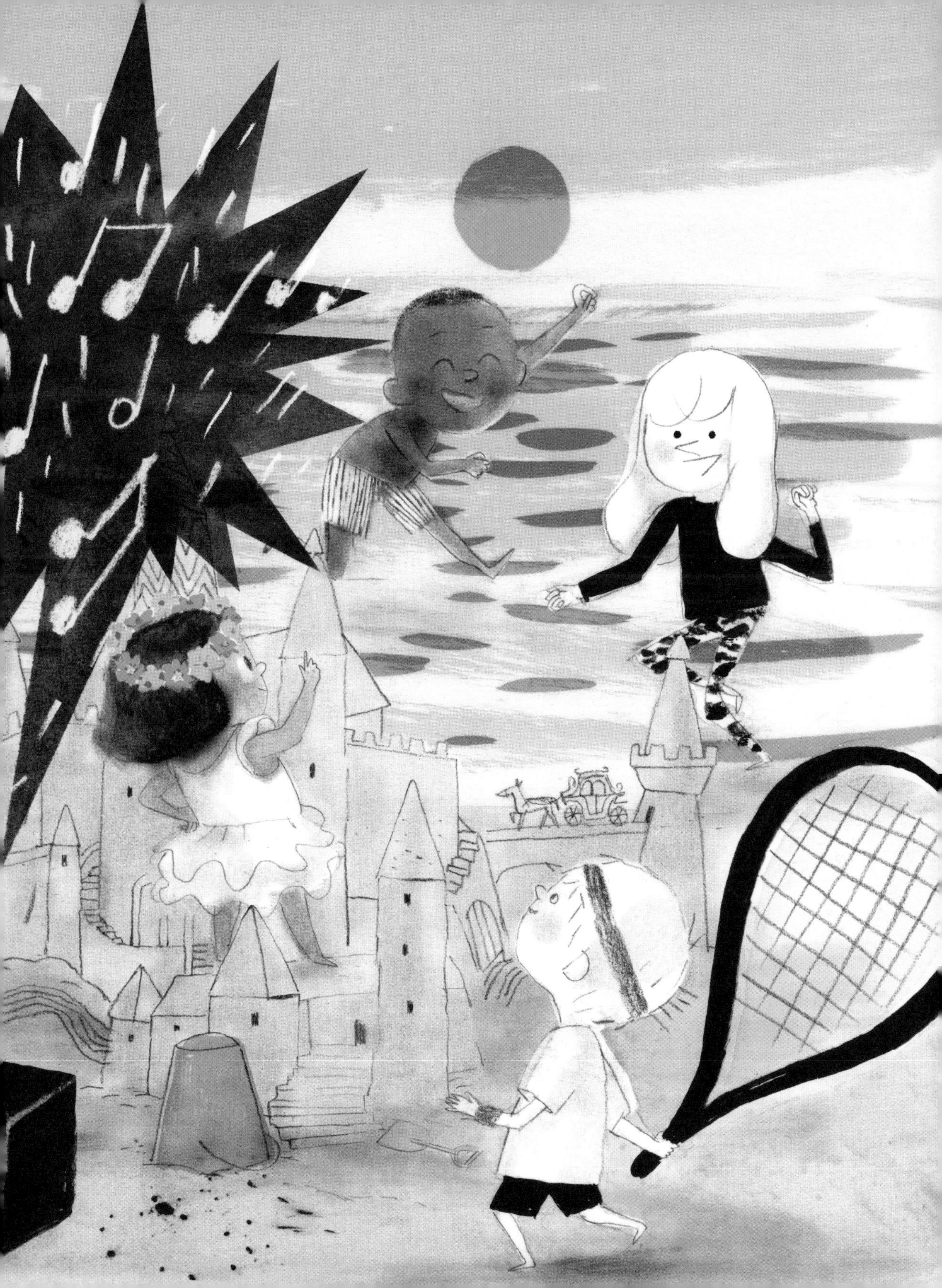

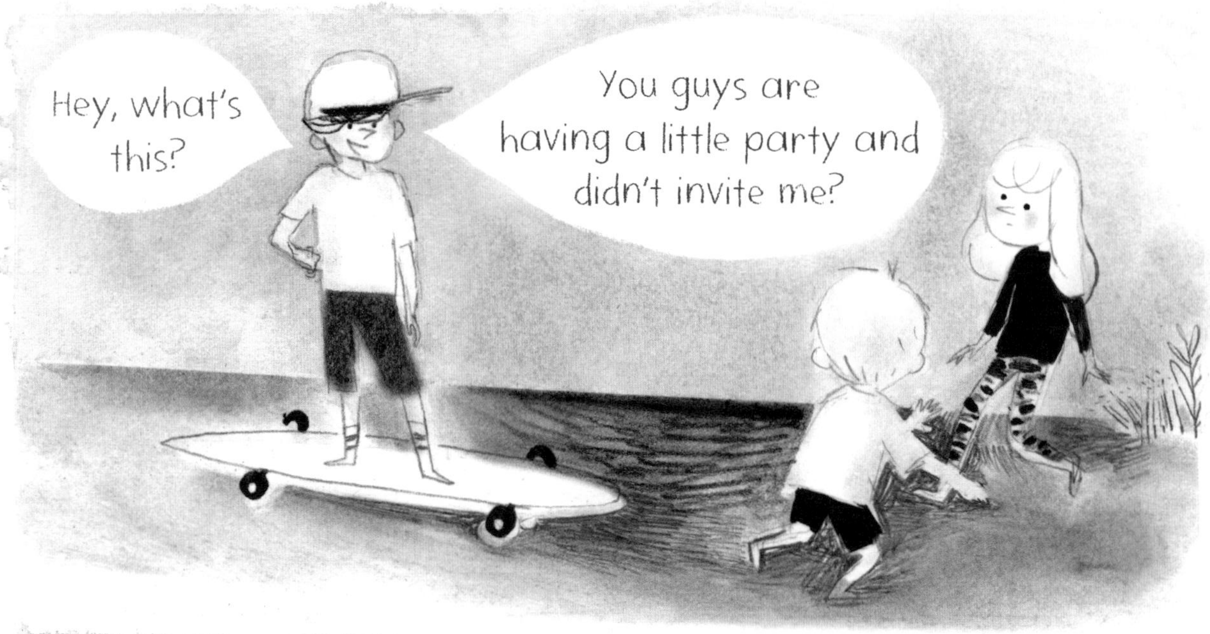
Hey, what's this?
You guys are having a little party and didn't invite me?
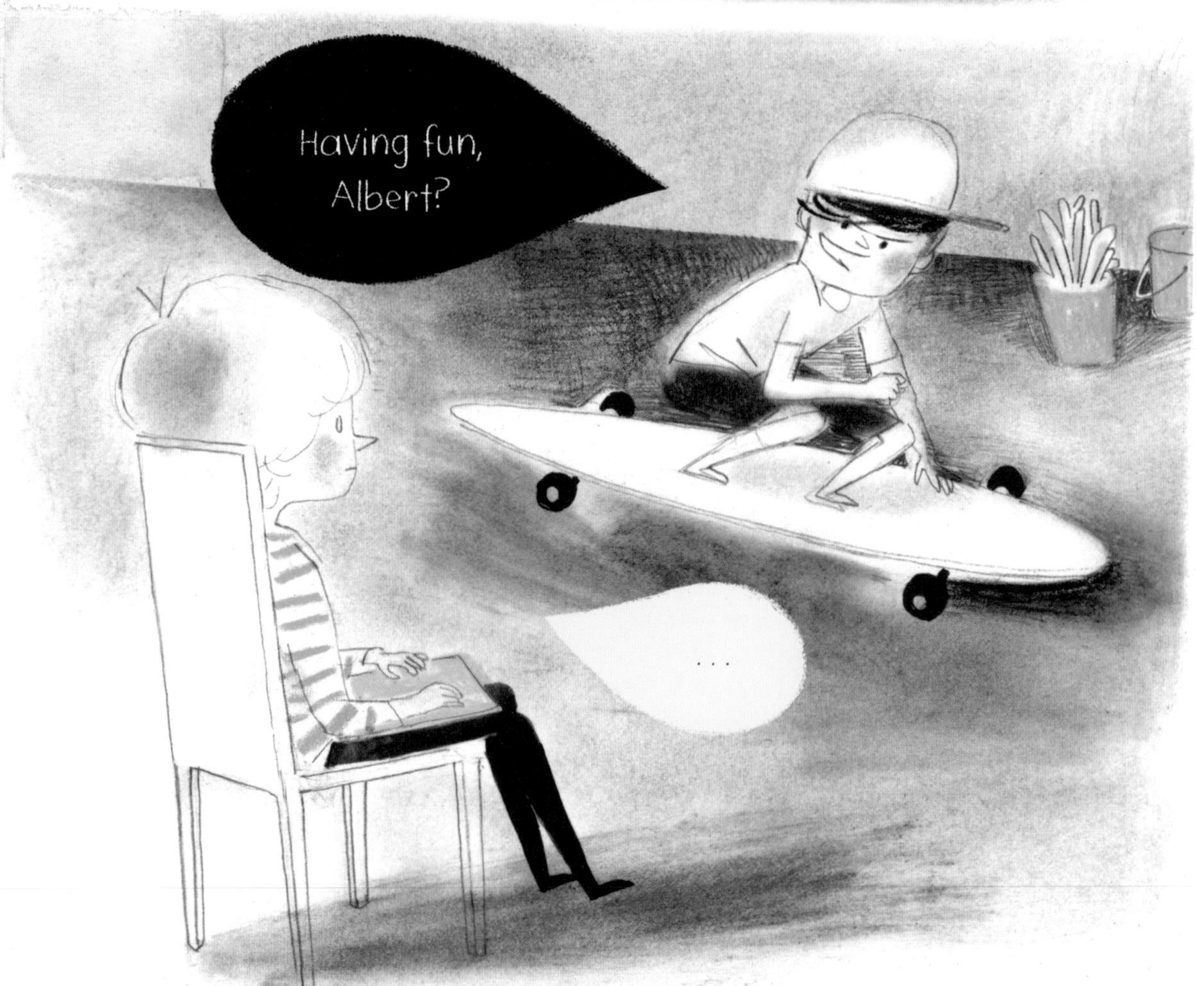
Having fun, Albert?
...

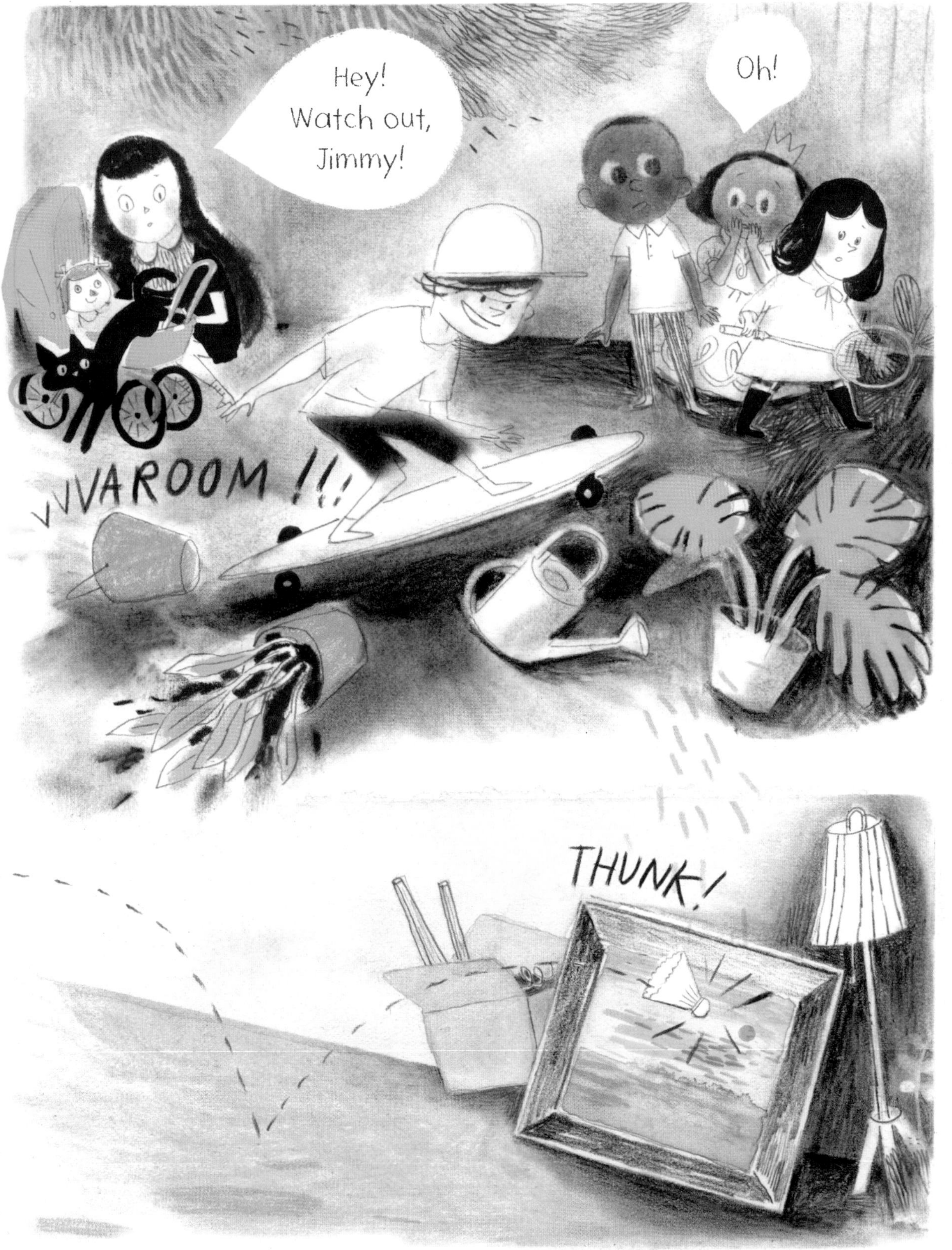
Hey! Watch out, Jimmy!
Oh!
VVVAROOM !!!
THUNK!

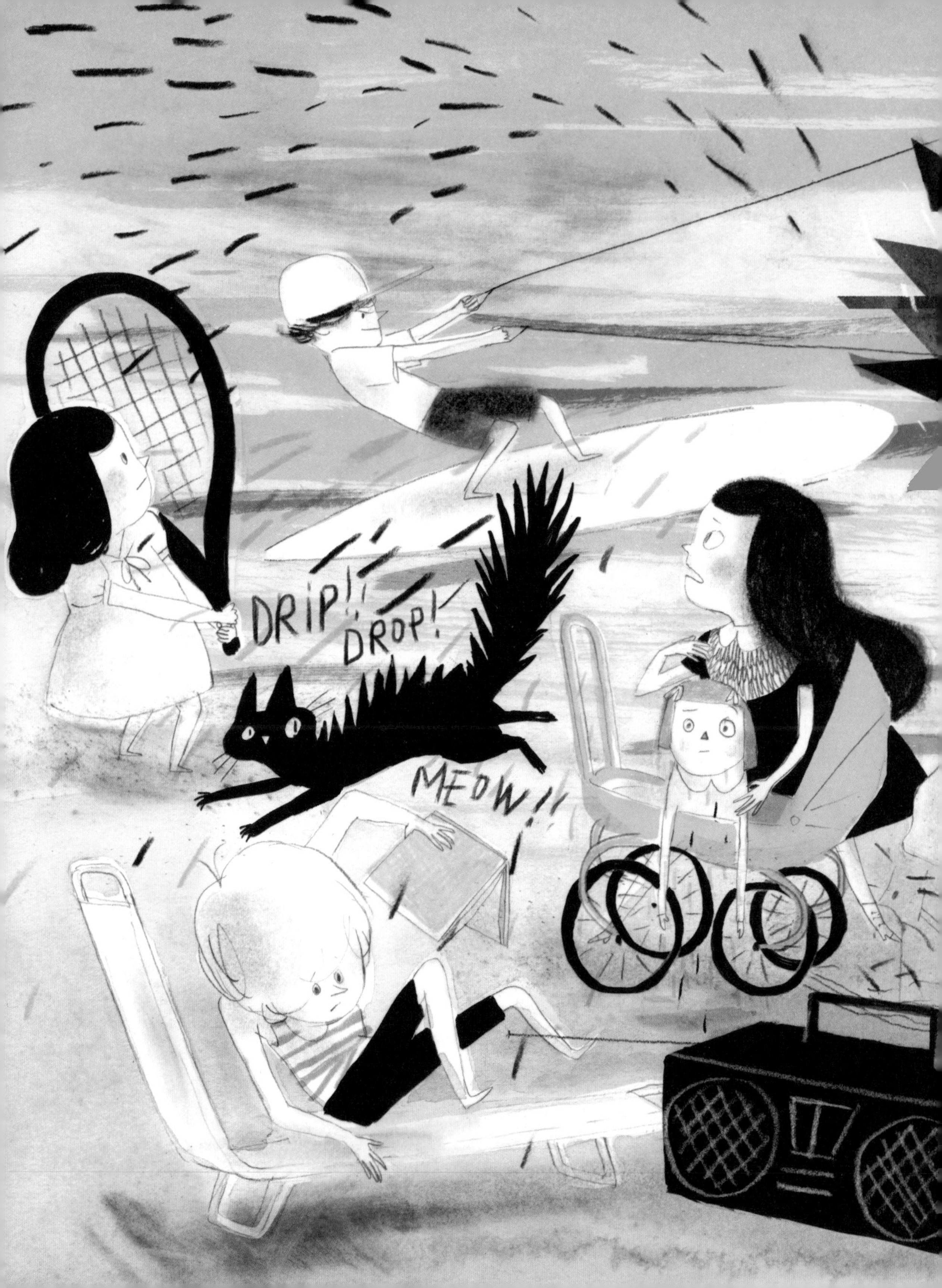
DRIP!
DROP!
MEOW!

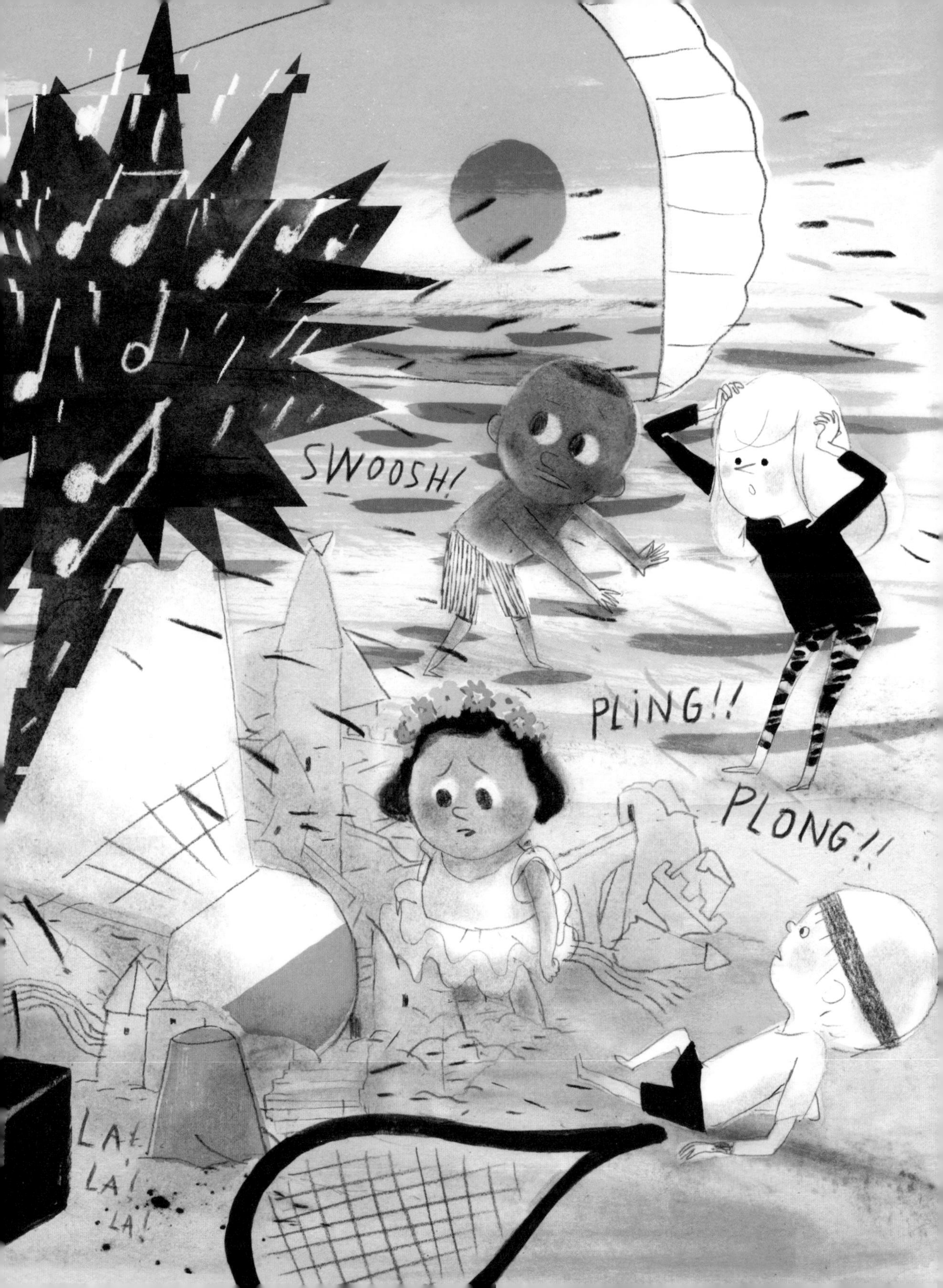
SWOOSH!
PLING!!
PLONG!!
LA!
LA!
LA!

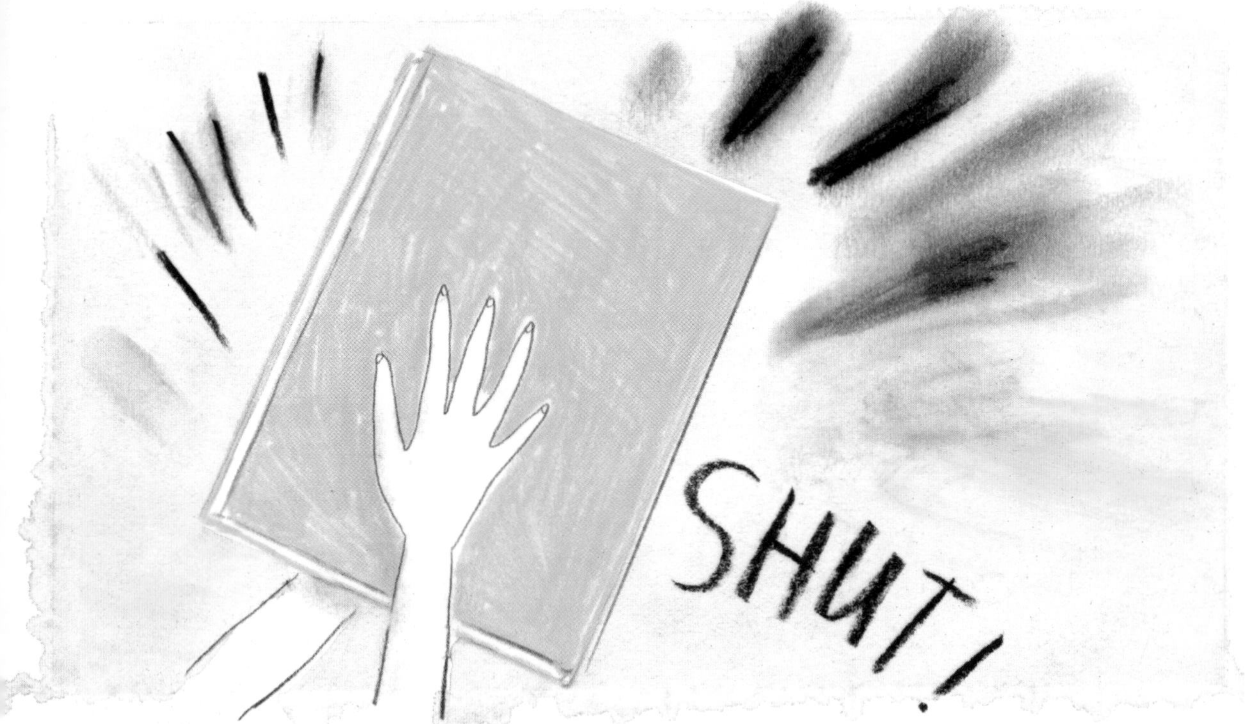
SHUT!

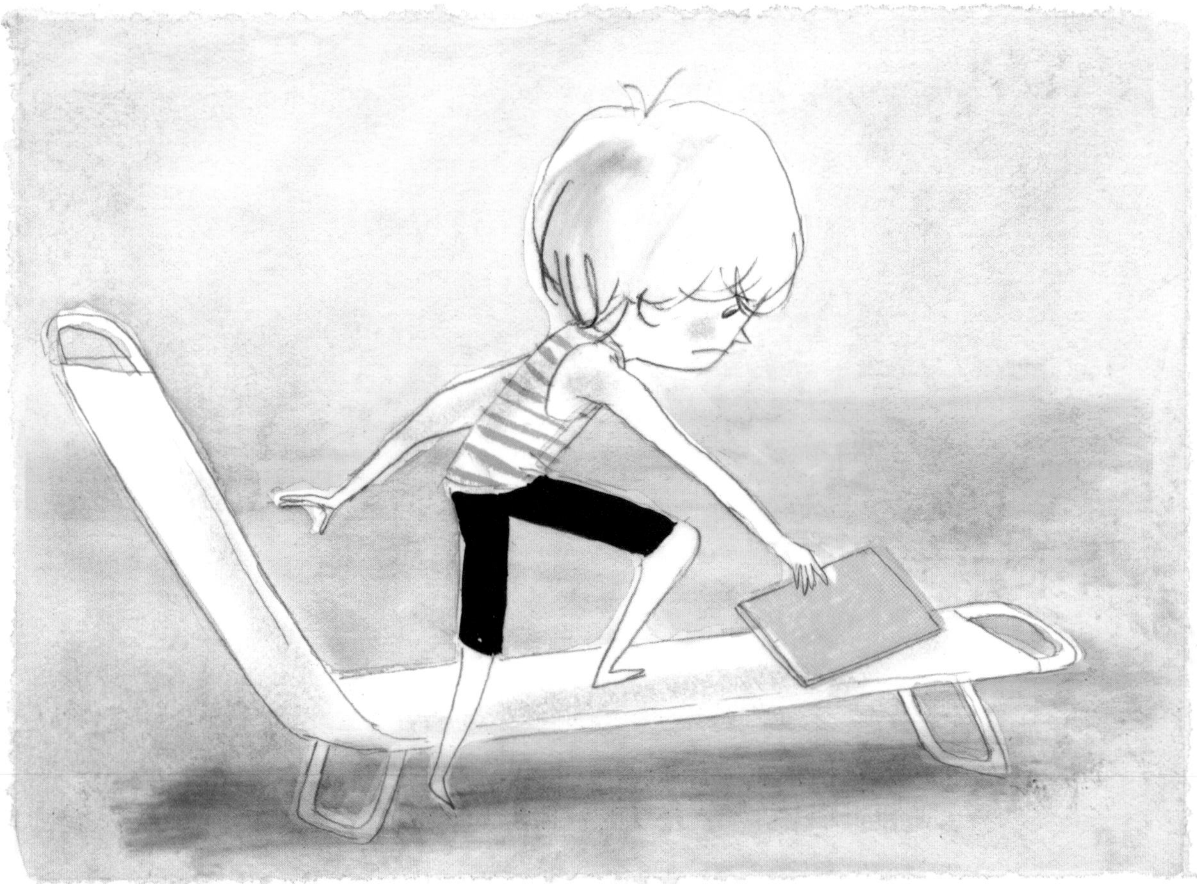

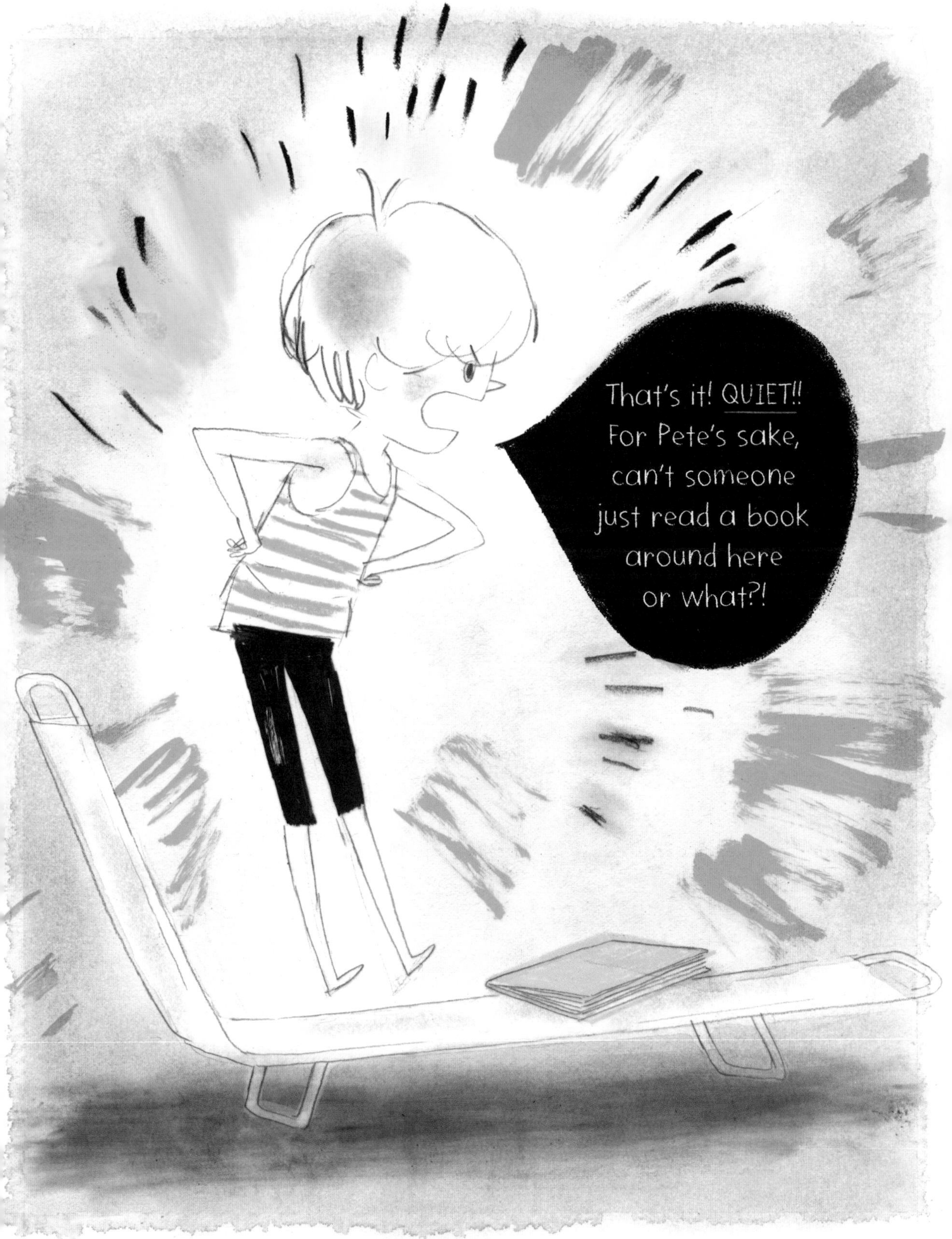
That's it! QUIET!! For Pete's sake, can't someone just read a book around here or what?!

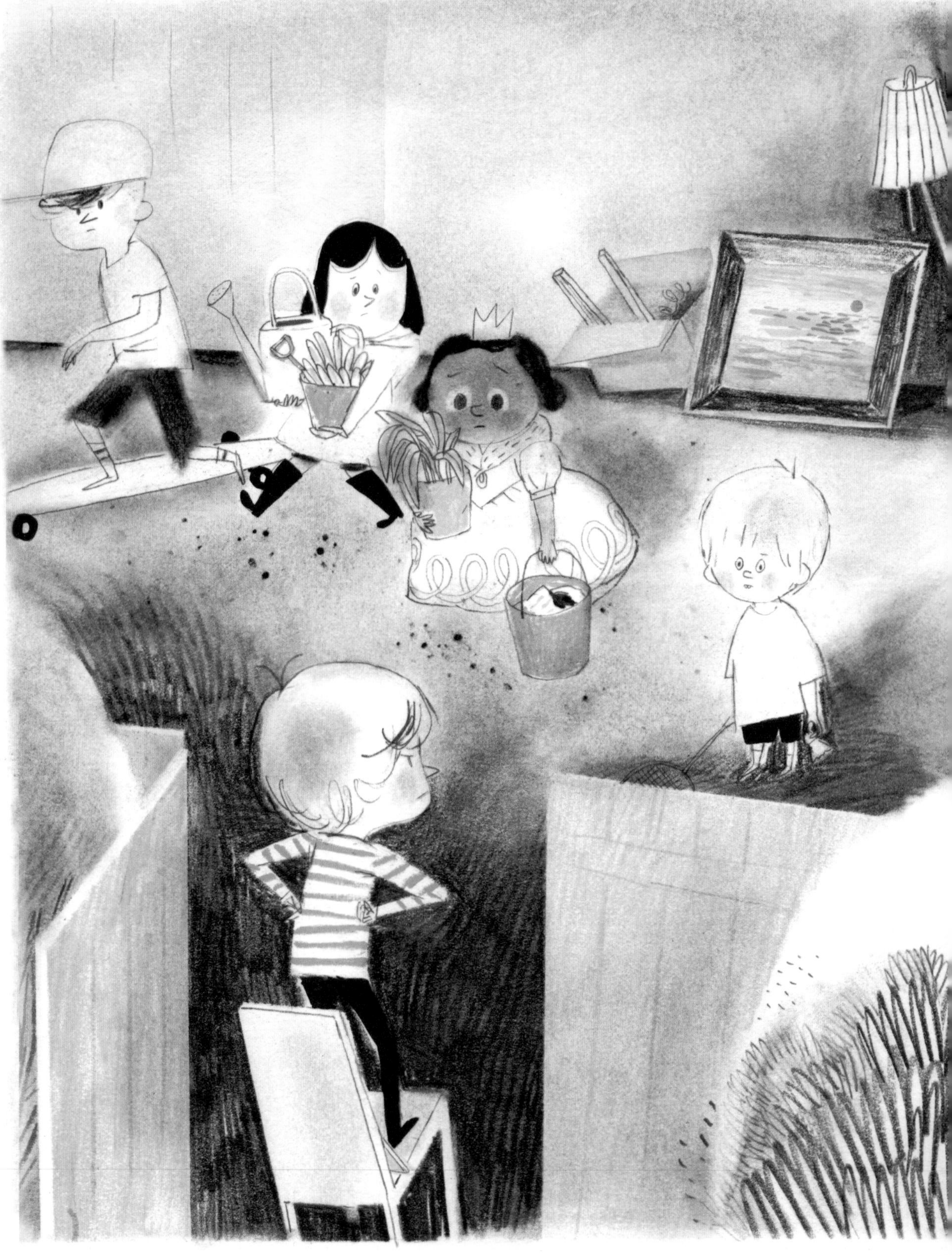

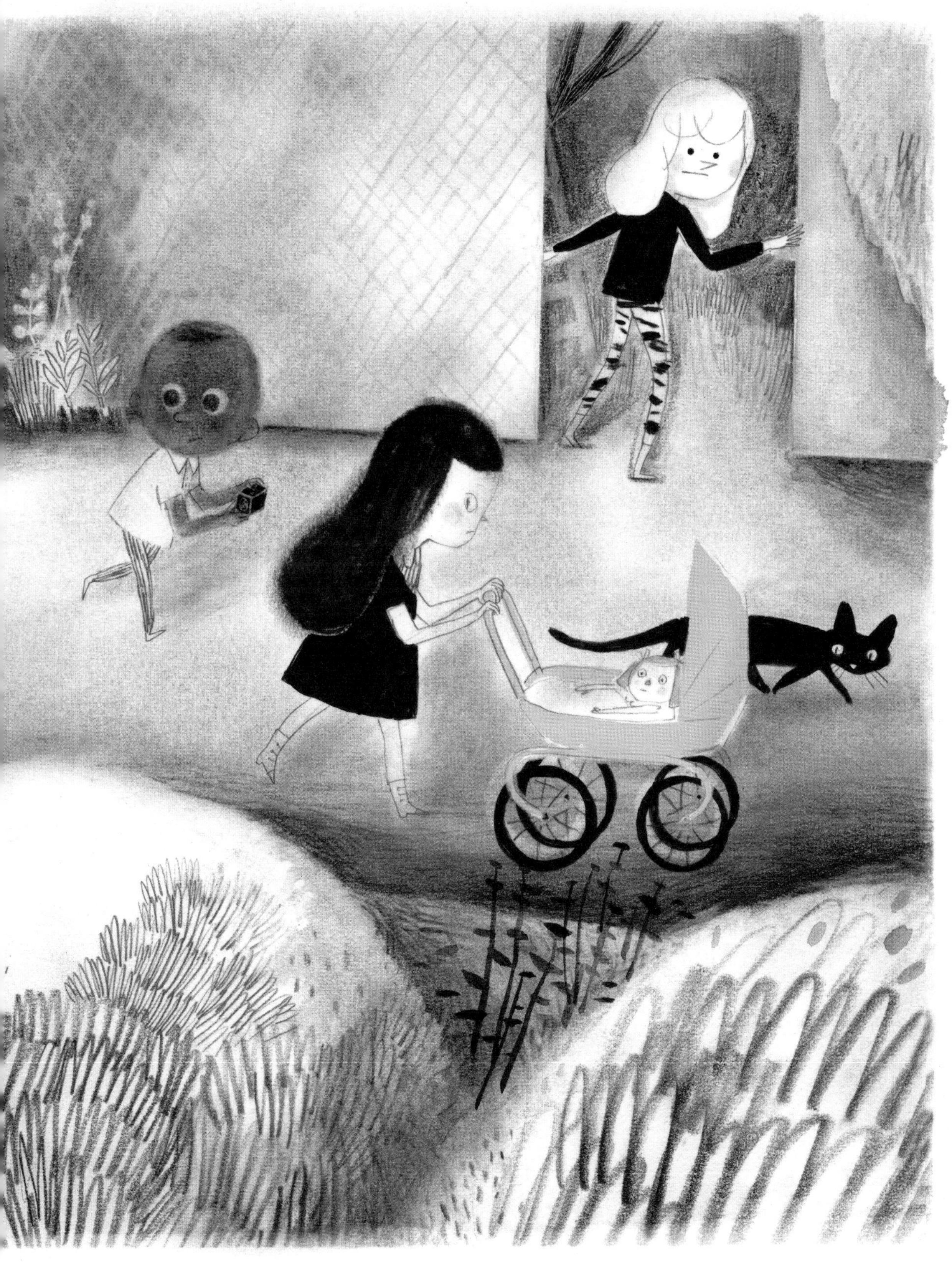

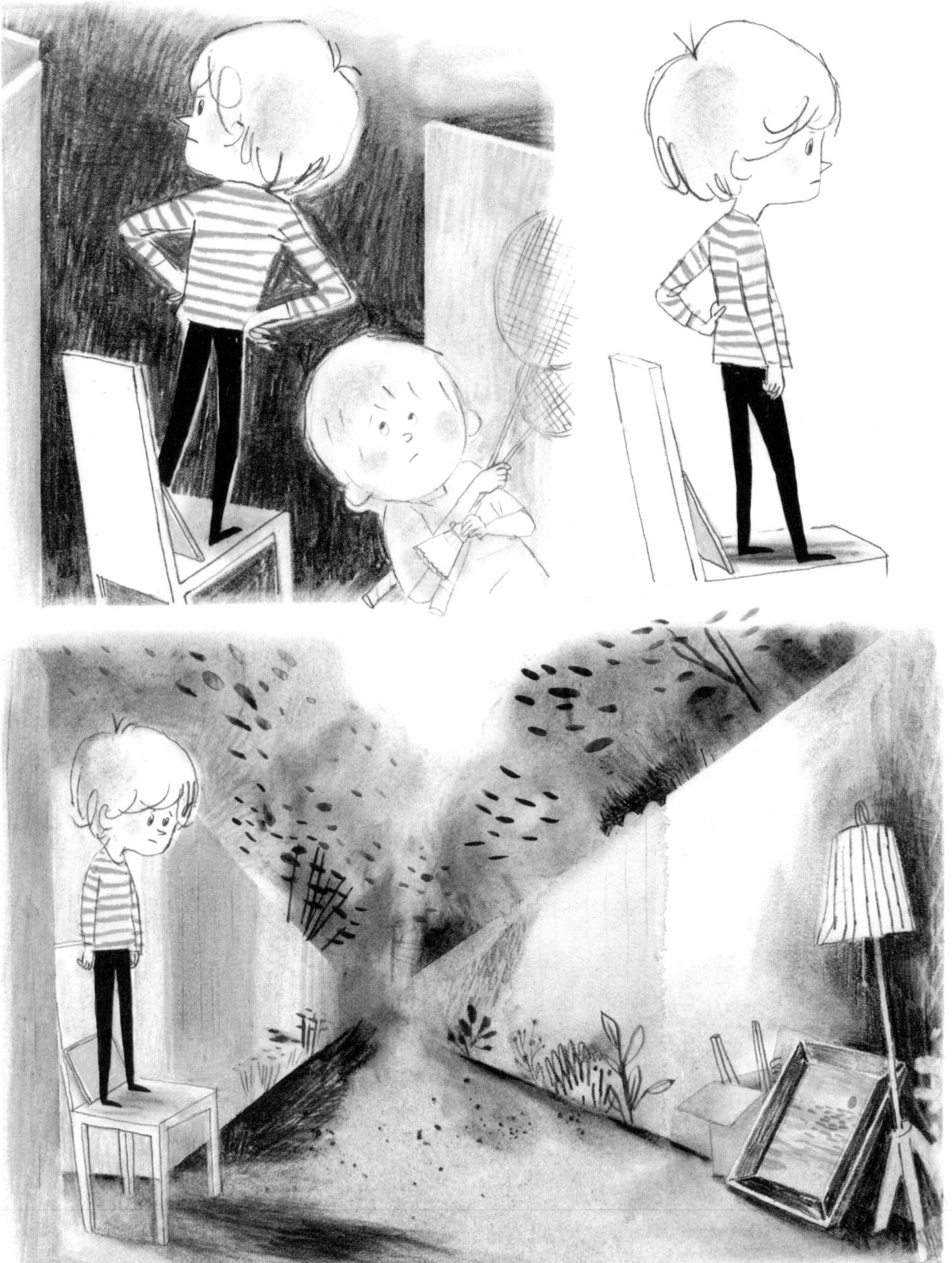

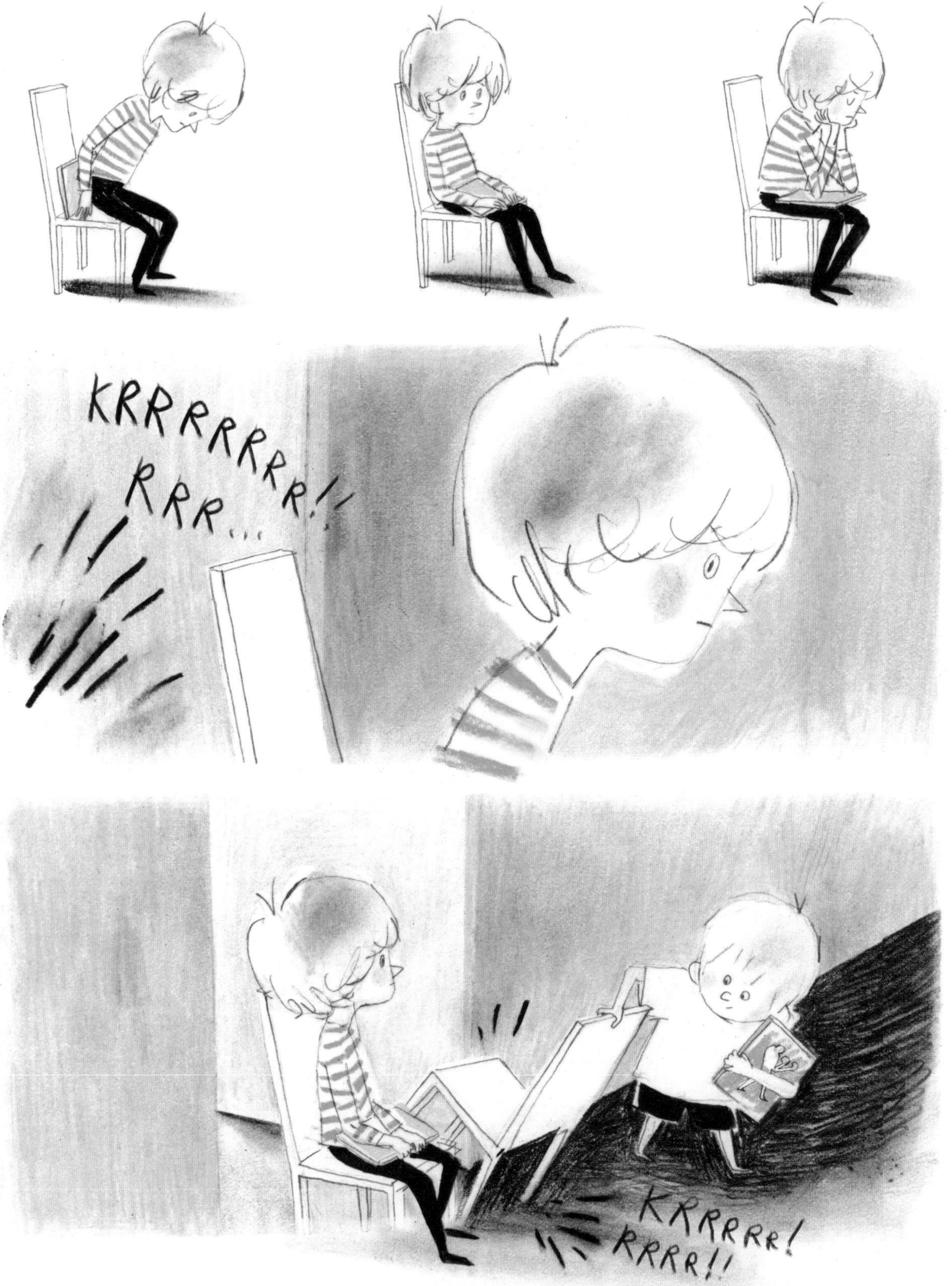
KRRRRRRRR!
RRR...
KRRRRRR!
RRRR!!

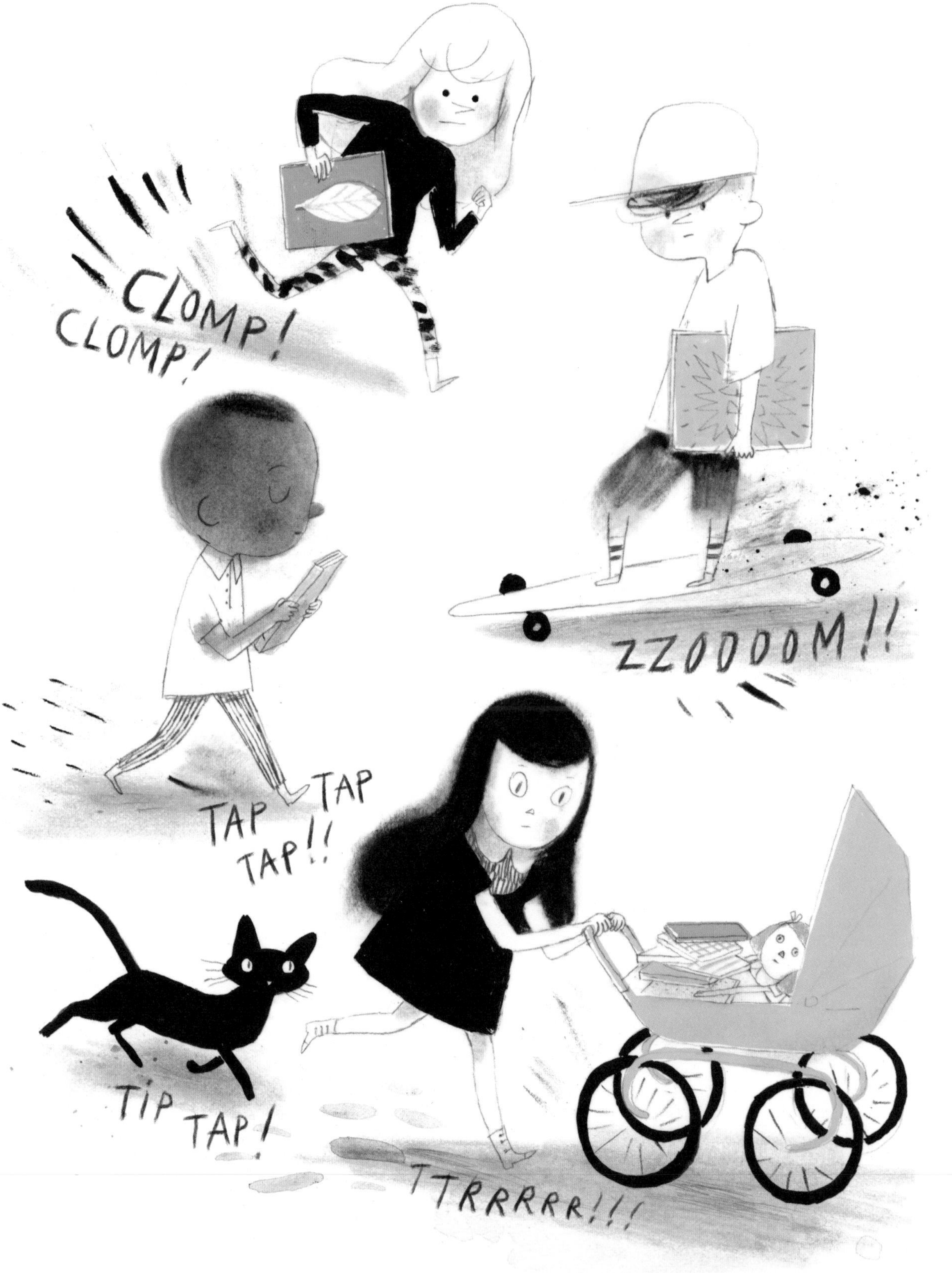
CLOMP!
CLOMP!
ZZOOOOOM!!
TAP
TAP
TAP!!
TIP TAP!
TTRRRRRR!!!

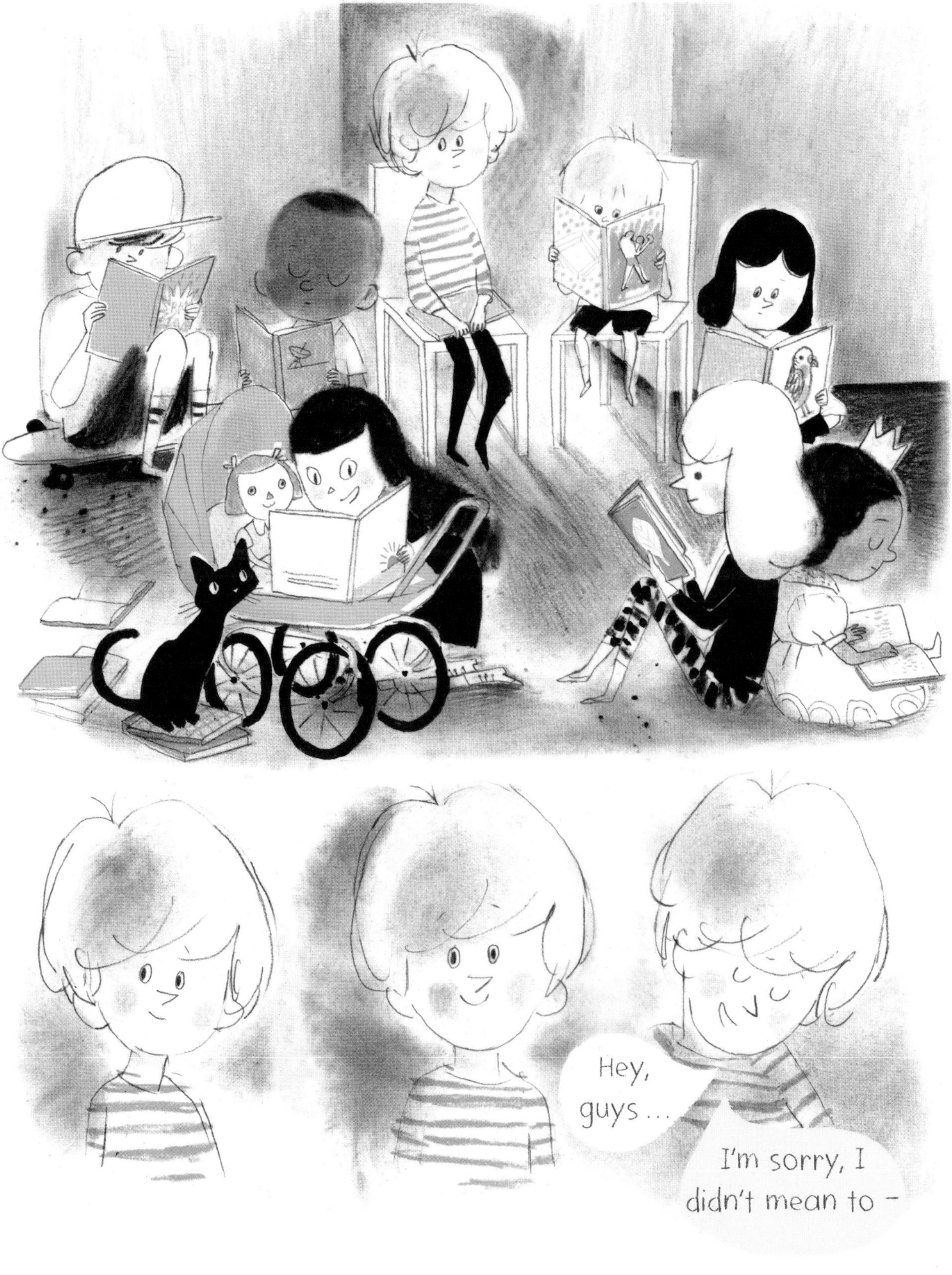
Hey, guys . . .
I'm sorry, I didn't mean to –

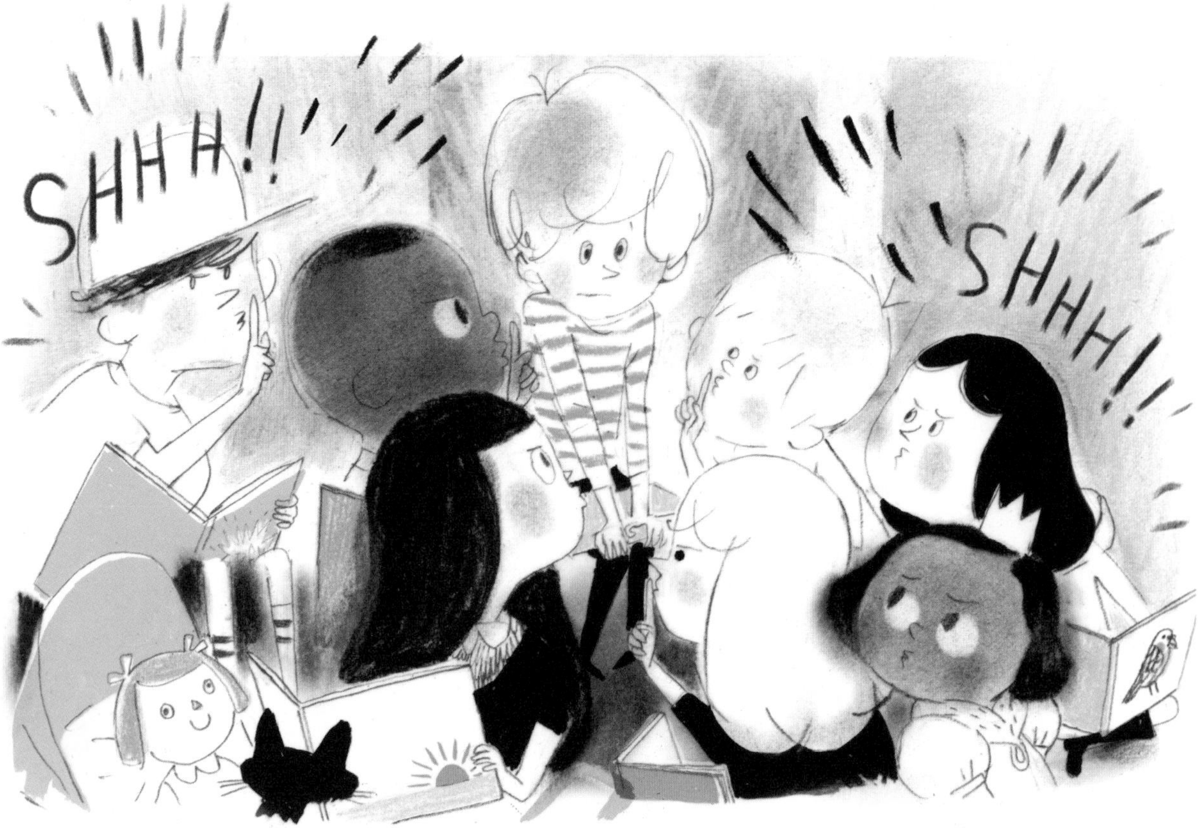
SHHH!!
SHHH!!

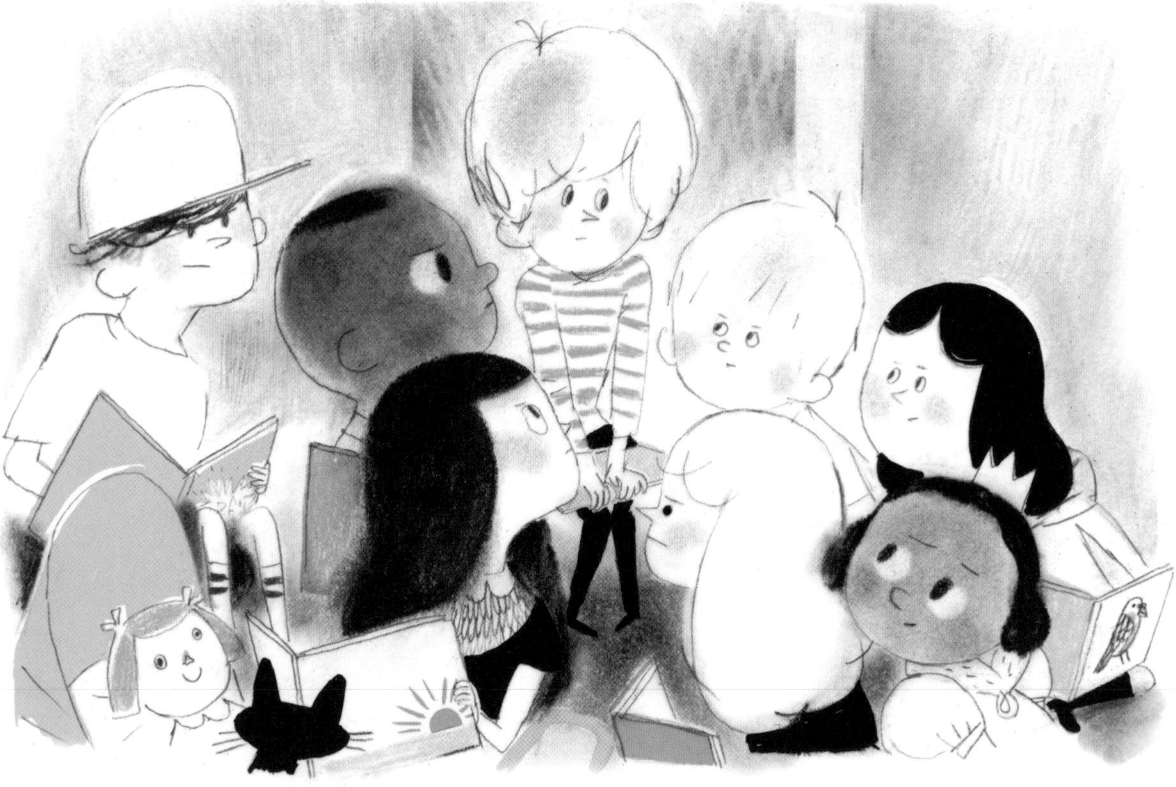

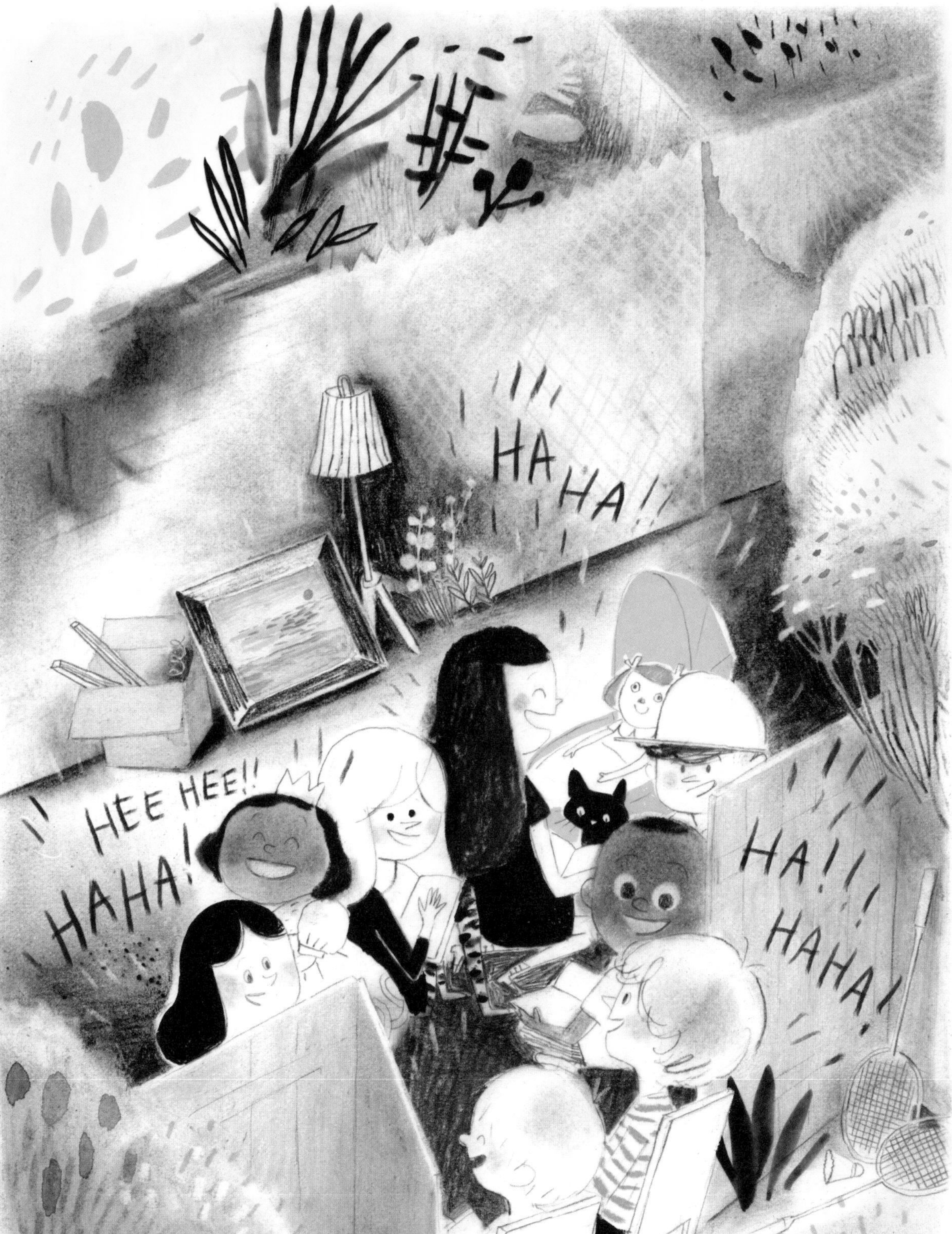
HA HA!
HEE HEE!!
HAHA!
HA!
HAHA!

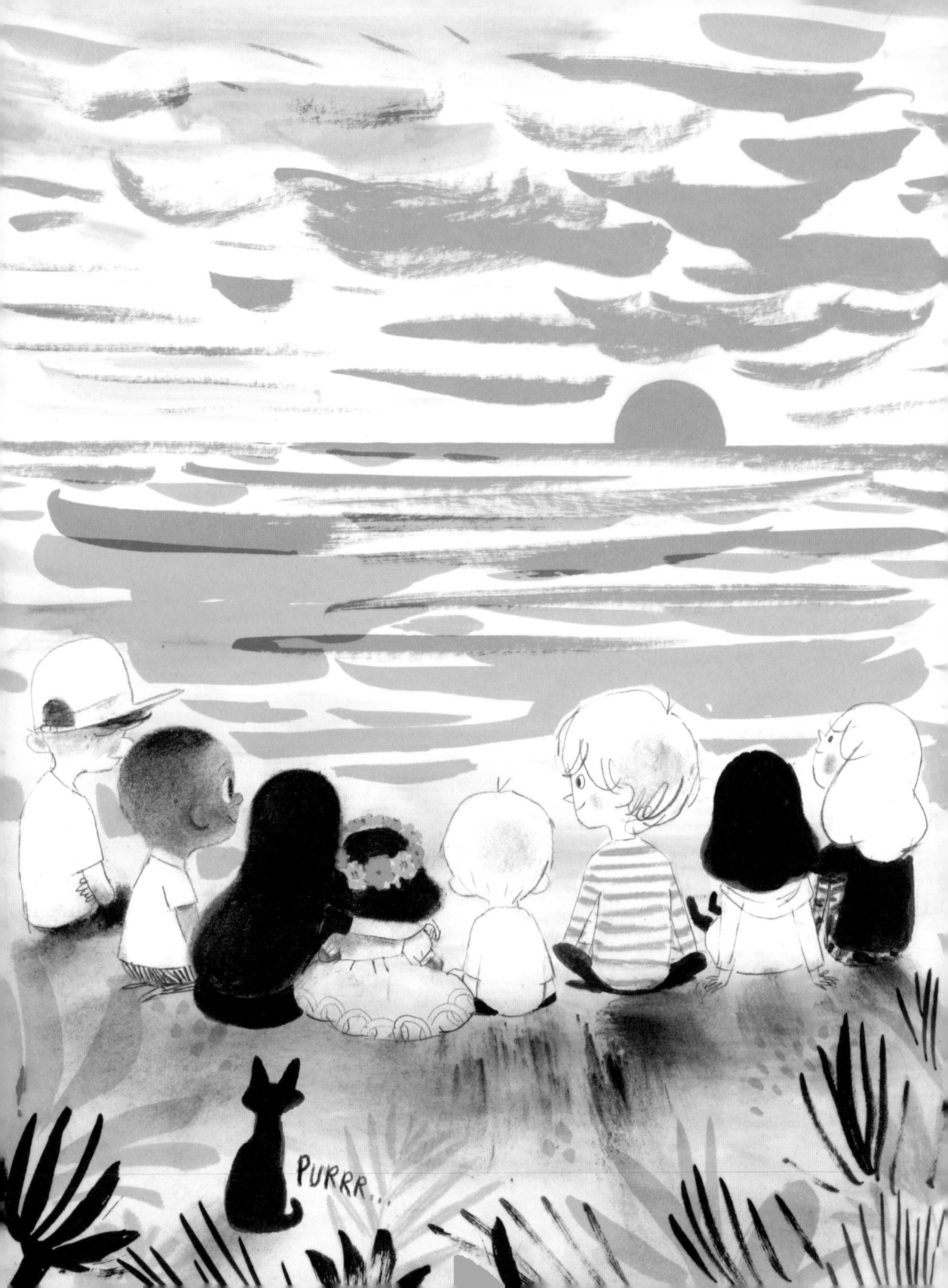
PURRR...

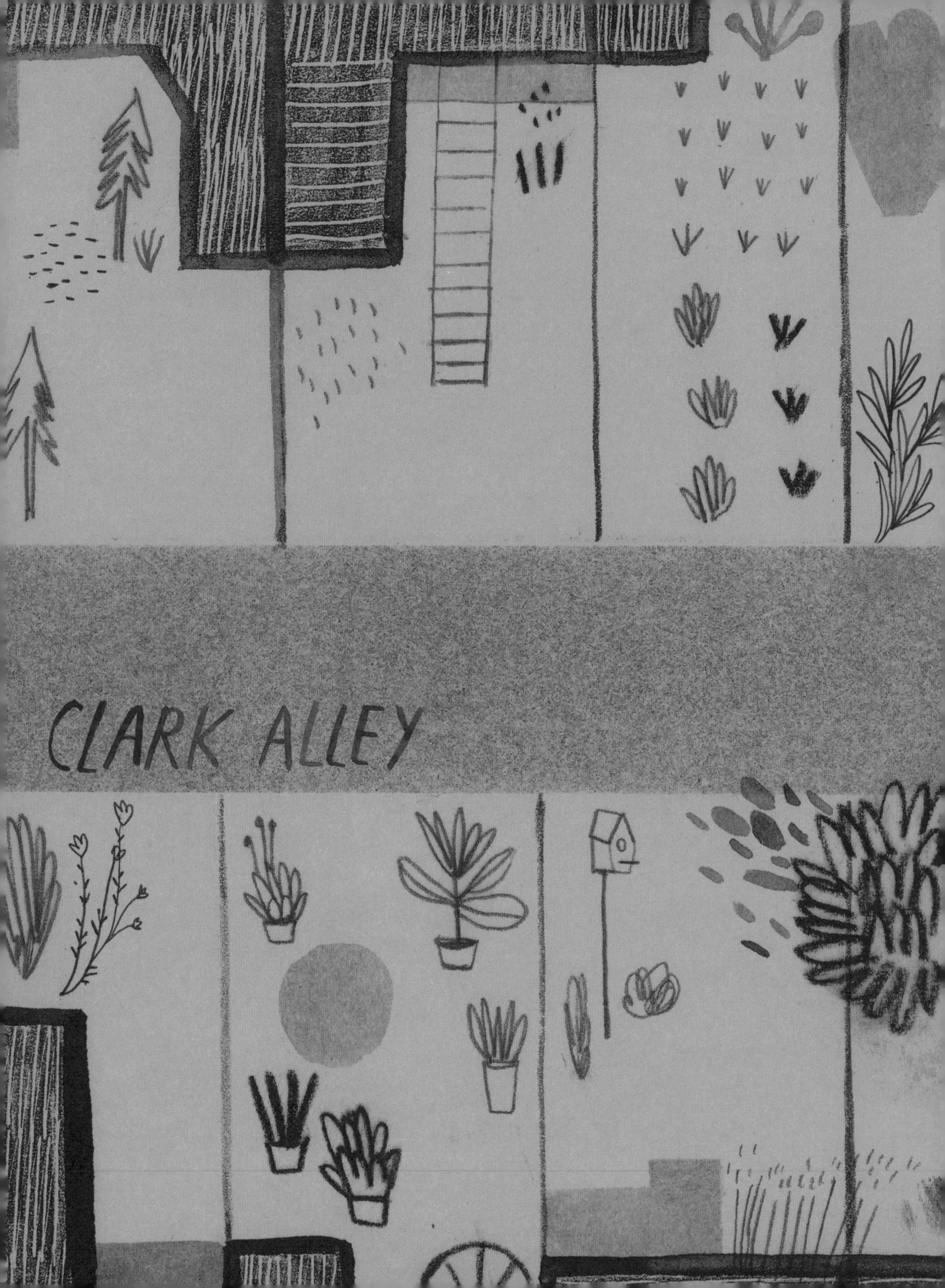
CLARK ALLEY